JOE COLTON'S JOURNAL

My second son, Drake, has always had a soft spot for Maya Ramirez. They were smitten with each other in their youth, but as an heir to the Colton fortune, my son kept his distance from the housekeeper's daughter. Back then, I encouraged his self-sacrifice, but I've learned a lot about love and loss over the years, and now I believe that some people are destined for each other. Like his mother and me—until Meredith turned her back on me and decided to make my life hell. But I digress.... When Drake—a Navy SEAL who often disappears to parts unknown for long periods of time—returned home for a brief visit several months ago, he finally gave in to his pent-up passion for Maya. Now she's pregnant, and my son insists she's about to give birth to a Colton baby! But my tight-lipped boy has his work cut out for him if he intends to stake a claim on his woman and child....

About the Author

LAURIE PAIGE

reports that in addition to remodeling the kitchen in her new (to her) mountain retreat home, she has adopted two mixed-breed Labrador retrievers. It's like having two two-year-olds in the house. She wishes she'd tossed in twin dogs that steal socks and hide them in different rooms in the house in the story of Maya and Drake. That would have added some confusing elements for the characters! On second thought, Drake probably had all the problems he could handle dealing with proud, stubborn Maya and claiming a place in her life and that of their child! However, true love can smooth out the most tangled of troubles...except for those caused by two seventy-pound dogs. In that case, Laurie recommends obedience classes, which is where she will be as soon as she finishes the next book.

The Housekeeper's Daughter

Laurie
Paige

Published by Silhouette Books
America's Publisher of Contemporary Romance

Special thanks and acknowledgment are given
to Laurie Paige for her contribution
to THE COLTONS series.

SILHOUETTE BOOKS
300 East 42nd St.,
New York, N. Y. 10017

ISBN 0-373-38710-5

THE HOUSEKEEPER'S DAUGHTER

Visit Silhouette at www.eHarlequin.com

Printed in U.S.A.

THE COLTONS

Meet the Coltons—
a California dynasty with a legacy of privilege and power.

Drake Colton: *Navy SEAL.* He'd come home to celebrate his father's sixtieth birthday, but this officer's family-filled agenda gives way to a night of passion when he is reunited with the housekeeper's daughter.

Maya Ramirez: *Overnight Cinderella.* Though Drake Colton had always seen her as a kid sister, this tomboy has blossomed into a raven-haired beauty in his absence. And one night, he makes all her adolescent fantasies a breathtaking reality!

Inez Ramirez: *Suspicious mother.* She and her husband have always been loyal to the Colton family but now she suspects that a certain Colton may be responsible for her daughter's "condition."

THE COLTONS

Theodore Colton m. 1940 Kay Barkley
1908–1954 — 1919–1954

Ed Barkley m. 1916 Betty Barkley
1895–1966 — 1899–1970

Meredith Portman
1949–

Joseph Colton
1941–

m. 1969

Graham Colton
1946–

m. 1970 Cynthia Turner
1941–

- Jackson, 1973–
- Liza, 1975–

Foster Children
- Chance Reilly, 1967–
- Tripp Calhoun, 1968–
- Rebecca Powell, 1968–
- Wyatt Russell, 1969–
- Blake Fallon, 1969–
- River James, 1970–
- *Emily Blair, 1980–

Natural Children
- Rand, 1970–
- Drake, 1972–
- Michael, 1972–1980
- Sophie, 1974–
- Amber, 1976–

Edna Kelly m. 1945 George Portman
1920–1970 — 1915–

Patsy
1949–

- Jewel, 1969–
  (by Ellis Mayfair)
- *Joe, Jr., 1991–
- *Teddy, Jr., 1993–

THE McGRATHS

Jack McGrath m. Maureen O'Toole
1906–1988 — 1915–1989

- Liam, 1936–
- Collin, 1938–
- Maude, 1940–
- Francis, 1942–
- Peter m. 1970 Andie Clifton
  1949– — 1951–
  - Austin, 1971–
  - Heather, 1976–

LEGEND
- - - Child of Affair
— Twins
* Adopted by Joe Colton

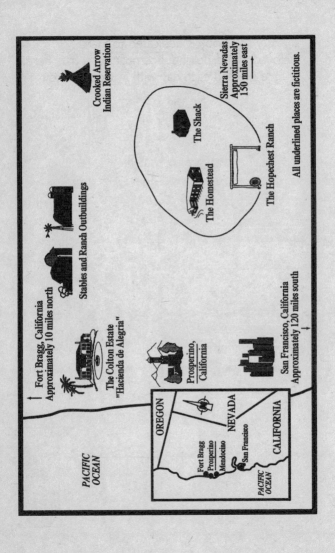

Crooked Arrow
Indian Reservation

Sierra Nevadas
Approximately
150 miles east

The Shack

Fort Bragg, California
Approximately 10 miles north

Stables and Ranch Outbuildings

The Homestead

The Hopechest Ranch

The Colton Estate
"Hacienda de Alegria"

All underlined places are fictitious.

Prosperino,
California

San Francisco, California
Approximately 120 miles south

PACIFIC
OCEAN

OREGON

NEVADA

CALIFORNIA

Fort Bragg
Prosperino
Mendocino
San Francisco

PACIFIC
OCEAN

This book is dedicated to Hartley,
beloved friend, delightful companion, a true hero.
He greeted each day with a "woof" of joy.

One

Maya Ramirez breathed deeply of the crystalline air and let it out in a long exhalation. The accompanying sigh was not exactly one of contentment—too many disturbing things had happened on the Colton ranch the past eight months for contentment to prevail—but at least she had found a certain peace of mind concerning her own future.

Her horse, a sweet mare named Penny for the coppery highlights of her coat, twitched one ear in her direction. Maya patted the mare's neck and admired the scenery.

It was one of those February days along the coast of northern California in which the sky gleamed a breath-catching blue and the temperature had soared into the sixties after a week of cold, drizzly rain. Today, the cloud bank had receded offshore and all was bright and beautiful. For the first time in months, anything seemed possible.

Almost anything, Maya corrected, batting away a lazy bee that hummed over the lupine that was already beginning to flower in stalks of white, yellow and lavender blue.

"A hawk," ten-year-old Joe Colton, Jr., yelled, pointing at the long, sweeping line of fifty-foot cliffs that scalloped the ocean along the western border of the ranch.

"Where?" Teddy Colton, younger by two years, called.

"Right there, silly— Uh, right there," Joe amended with a quick glance at Maya.

She gave him an approving nod, then smiled with affection. She didn't allow name-calling or insults. Although newly employed as their full-time nanny, she'd been baby-sitting the boys for years, being only sixteen when she'd first been asked to accompany Mrs. Colton to a spa and take care of Joe Junior, who had been a baby at the time.

Ten years ago. Maya sighed and shifted in the saddle, the sudden sting of tears surprising her as she contemplated the passage of time—so fast and yet so slow.

When Mrs. Colton had had Teddy, Maya had helped out with him, too. After graduating from the local high school, she'd started college via computer courses and worked on the Colton estate when needed by her mother, who was the housekeeper there.

Last month she'd been asked to move into the main house and take over as a full-time baby-sitter for the two youngest Colton boys. The nanny, Ms. Meredith called her. Frowning, Maya admitted she'd needed the job rather desperately.

She swatted another bee out of her face, then noticed several others crawling in Penny's mane. The mare shook her head as one landed on her ear. Maya realized the warm weather had caused a swarm.

"Can we race?" Teddy shouted, giving her an appealing glance from his blue eyes.

She nodded. "I think we're running into a swarm of bees. Turn back toward the ranch and ease into a canter. Don't swat the bees. They'll fly off if you leave them alone and don't scare them."

Both boys glanced around anxiously, but they kept their heads and did as told. After making sure they were on their way, she turned the mare, who switched her tail to each side and shook her head again. Gently Maya urged the mare into a fast walk, then past a trot into a loping run.

In front of her, the brothers let out a whoop of excitement and raced toward the stable in the distance. She leaned forward with a grimace and tightened her knees, but she couldn't keep up the pace. After reining the mare back to a fast walk, she relaxed once more.

The mare repeatedly shook her head as they neared the paddock. Her ears twitched nervously.

Maya patted her on the neck. "Hey, pretty Penny, what's the matter, girl? The bees are gone—"

She got no further when the horse gave a startled whinny, tossed her head and, without warning, took off at a dead run toward the stable. Maya grabbed the saddle horn and held on for dear life, fear rushing over her as she thought of falling.

The adrenaline boost gave her the strength to rise in the stirrups so that her weight shifted to her legs and her thighs acted as shock absorbers during the wild ride across the pasture. She pulled on the reins, but the mare raced on, heedless of the rider's commands.

Ahead of her, she saw the boys dismount and stare at her in confusion. Then a man leaped on the horse Joe had been riding and raced toward her.

Maya saw the fence looming fifty yards in front of her and knew she would never make the jump. Neither would the mare with the extra weight of a rider and saddle on her back. "Whoa," she called desperately and pulled on the reins to turn the frightened horse to the side.

Hearing hoofbeats coming up behind her, she glanced over her shoulder. The other rider was circling toward them. He closed in and raced alongside her.

"Kick free and come to me," he yelled.

She slid her feet out of the stirrups and leaped into his arms just as he reached for her. He turned his mount and they ran alongside the fence. Penny fell in behind them and followed. Gradually he slowed his horse, then stopped.

In the stillness, there was only the sound of the two horses and the two humans, panting from the wild exertion of the run. His arms enclosed her in a blanket of safety.

It was like coming home.

"What the hell were you thinking, riding like that in your condition?" Drake Colton demanded, his golden-brown eyes flashing like molten rock in the afternoon sun, his gaze hot with fury.

So much for illusions. "I think my horse got a bee in her ear," Maya said defensively, fighting a ridiculous urge to burst into tears now that the danger was over.

She was pressed to his chest in a vise grip. His heart pounded against hers, which was also beating hard with the aftermath of the fear when her horse bolted and with a new fear as his eyes raked down her figure.

She struggled to push away from his heat and his anger, the vibrant masculinity that called to something equally vibrant inside her. "I can walk," she told him, forcing herself to ignore the unruly needs that clamored for attention inside her.

Memories of lying snug in his arms for hours and hours overcame common sense—the warmth of his embrace, the way his hands moved on her, his sudden smile. She closed her eyes and foolishly wished for things that were never going to happen. But a person could dream....

Drake returned to the stable. There, he let her gently slide to the ground, then dropped down beside her. "Here, boys, take care of the horses."

Drake's two youngest brothers, big-eyed with worry, took the reins, then stood there and looked from their older brother to their nanny as if afraid to leave them alone.

"I'm not going to hurt her," Drake assured them in harsh tones, then added for her ears alone, "yet."

"Ask River to check Penny's ear. I think she was stung by one of the bees," Maya called to the youngsters, ignoring the threat from the furious man beside her as the fears and dreams, the need to cry, faded into fatalistic calm.

She had thought this moment might come someday. But not so soon. She wasn't ready, hadn't prepared....

After the boys led the horses off to the stable, Drake turned back to Maya. It hurt to look at her, at the thick, dark splendor of her hair, the endless depths of her brown eyes and most of all, at the protruding mound of her tummy.

"Just how pregnant are you, anyway?" he demanded, which wasn't at all what he'd planned to say to her upon his arrival at the ranch thirty minutes ago. At that time, he'd planned a calm, reasonable approach to their problems.

"What do you care?" she asked, so softly he almost didn't hear. Then she walked away without a backward glance, leaving him standing in the dust, his heart pounding with emotions he couldn't describe.

Maya stood under the shower and let the water flow over her from head to toes. She washed, rinsed and stepped out. From the hallway, she heard a knock on her door.

"Just a minute," she called.

Fear coiled through her, not a pounding fear as earlier, but fear just the same. She wondered what ill fortune had brought Drake back to the ranch at this time.

Along with her bodily changes, her emotions had become all topsy-turvy during the past few months. That afternoon had been the worst. Yearning, joy, grief—she'd experienced all those and more during the minutes he'd held her close in that rock-solid embrace, their hearts beating as one.

As they had last summer.

But this wasn't summer, she reminded herself. Summer and fall had come and gone with no word from him. Her confusion was to be expected; she'd thought she would also be gone before Drake came around again.

There's no place in my life for a wife and family, his curt farewell note had stated.

Pain, as fresh, as unbelievable, as the morning she'd read those words, scorched through her, but there was no time for it now. She pulled on a terry-cloth robe and wrapped a towel around her hair. Her hands were trembling.

"Maya?"

Relief surged through her as she realized her mother was at the door. Inez Ramirez had been housekeeper at the Hacienda de Alegria ranch since before Maya was born. Maya's father was the gardener and general groundskeeper.

"Come on in. The door's open," Maya invited.

Her mother looked her over when she entered. "Teddy said you nearly took a spill while you were riding."

"Penny bolted. I think she got stung in the ear. But I'm fine. Drake rescued me." She smiled to alleviate her mother's worries.

"I heard. The boys said River found the stinger and removed it." Inez closed the door and crossed the room to lay a hand on her daughter's forehead. "You don't feel dizzy or faint? No pain anywhere?"

"No, really, I'm quite all right."

Her mother ignored her. "Maybe you should see the doctor. I can drive you to town."

"That won't be necessary. I go in for my monthly checkup Tuesday. That's only two more days. I don't want to bother the doctor on a Sunday."

Inez sighed and backed off. "If you start hurting, call me right away. Or if your water breaks."

"I will."

Maya watched her mother retrace her steps to the door, ready to return to the kitchen to prepare the evening meal for the Colton family, and whoever else might be in residence.

Her parents had been wonderful to her, after getting past the first shock of her news that she was expecting. They had immediately assumed she and Andy Martin, a local math teacher, would be marrying soon. They had been even more shocked when she'd had to tell them that Andy, the man she'd been seeing regularly until a few months ago, wasn't the father.

Andy was her friend, but he wasn't her lover.

Alone once more, Maya crossed her arms over her abdomen and silently prayed that Drake wouldn't discover she was eight months pregnant with his child.

She thought of summer and starry nights and the

blossoming of hot, wild passion that had known no bounds. They had made love in her bed, in his, in the sweet-smelling, prickly hay stored in the stable and barn.

After they'd danced several times at his father's birthday party, Drake had made a quick trip to Prosperino, the tiny town that served the ranchers and dairy farmers and tourists who stayed at the many bed-and-breakfast inns along the coast around here. His dark, smoldering glances had told her why the trip was necessary—birth control.

But they hadn't made love that night. During the toast to Joe Colton in celebration of his sixtieth birthday, someone had shot at the Colton patriarch. The ranch had been in an uproar for hours, the police milling about and questioning everyone over and over. No one had gone to bed until daybreak.

However, there had been other nights. "I'll take care of you," he'd said just before they'd made love. "Don't worry about anything."

And she had believed him.

She would have laughed at how foolish she'd been, except she felt too raw, too vulnerable at this moment and might end in tears. She wouldn't go to the table with weepy eyes and increase her parents' worry over her.

Knowing she had to, she rose, squared her shoulders and dressed. She would be expected to join the ranch staff who ate in the big dining area at one end of the kitchen. As someone had once remarked, life goes on.

The Colton family and friends usually ate in the

formal dining room or in the sunroom that separated the living room from the patio cupped in the center of the U-shaped house. Drake would be with them, so she wouldn't have to face him on top of everything else.

She dried her hair, pushed it back with butterfly clips and checked that her two charges were ready for dinner. They, too, were relegated to the kitchen now during meals, except for special occasions when their mother wanted to show them off.

Maya suppressed the cynical thought about her employer. The Coltons paid her salary as well as her tuition to college. Another few months and she would have a degree in early childhood education. Then she would take her child and leave the ranch.

Her heart gave a painful lurch at the thought of going away from all she knew and loved. Her parents would miss her. So would the boys. She would miss all of them dreadfully. However, she was twenty-six, old enough to make her own way in the world without depending on anyone.

When she, Joe Junior and Teddy entered the kitchen, an instant silence fell over the group gathered there. Glancing around, her eyes met the golden ones of her nemesis. "What are you doing here?" she blurted.

Heat rushed into her face at the quick stares she received from the house staff. He was a Colton. He could eat anywhere he pleased.

"Waiting for my brothers," he explained easily. "I wanted to thank them for their help this afternoon."

"Huh, it wasn't anything," Joe said. "You're the one who saved Maya."

"Yeah," Teddy agreed. "You were really quick. Can you teach me to jump on a horse like that, without using the stirrup to get up?"

Drake laughed, his teeth flashing white against his deeply tanned skin. "You only need to grow another few inches and you'll have no trouble."

The boys, tall and rangy for their ages as all the Colton men were, claimed seats on either side of their older brother, their eyes filled with admiration as they gazed at him. Drake stood and pulled out a chair on the other side of Teddy for her. When he was seated again, the boys asked a thousand questions about his life in the SEALs.

"Where ya been this time?" Joe asked.

"Central America."

"I wish I could go there," Teddy said, envious.

"No, you don't," Drake told him. "It was hot, the mosquitoes were as big as magpies and I had the boniest donkey God ever created to ride over the mountains."

He told funny stories during the meal, distracting them from the dangerous nature of his duties with the elite unit. Maya wondered what new scars he might have on his strong, lithe body.

Immediately, visions of his six-one, sinewy frame flooded her mind. She'd touched him all over, discovering every mole, every tiny imperfection...and every scar that spoke of a life lived dangerously close to the edge.

There's no place in my life...

He'd made love to her, then written those words as she lay sleeping, innocently believing in a future that included them and their children and a lifetime of sharing. The table blurred. She held the anguish in by dint of will. No one would see her cry, she had vowed eight months ago, after that first awful storm of grief had passed.

She ate the delicious meal without tasting it. Every time her eyes met Drake's over Teddy's blond curls, a shiver rushed through her. His gaze boded no good for her.

Drake stood at the window of his dark room and stared at the windows across the central courtyard patio. Maya's room. He knew it well. Once it had been his.

A flurry of emotion ran through him. Need. Anger. Despair. Loneliness. Name it and he'd felt it during the past eight months, even during hot nights in the humid jungles of Central America when he should have been concentrating on the business at hand.

His mission: rescue an American diplomat kidnapped by drug dealers and held in a mountain stronghold. He'd nearly lost two good men on that trek, but in the end, the mission had been a success.

A new scar from a bullet wound suddenly throbbed in the fleshy tissue of his hip. He'd been lucky. The bullet had missed his pelvic bone by half an inch. With a shattered hip, he wouldn't have made it out.

He laughed silently, sardonically. Yeah, he led a charmed life. There was just one problem at present. Maya.

Past emotions hadn't held a candle to the ones he'd felt upon seeing her on a runaway horse. Fear had clawed its way to his throat and stayed there until she was safe and secure in his arms.

Safe?

From her condition, she obviously hadn't been very safe in his arms eight months ago.

The irony of the note he'd left on the table beside her bed struck him. He'd told her his job was too dangerous, his life too busy, to include a wife.

Right. What about including a child? He shook his head, unable to answer that question just yet.

Staring at the window across the way, he set his jaw and headed out. It was time they had a serious talk. He entered the long hall running along the other wing of the house and rapped on the door.

Every nerve in Maya's body jumped when the knock sounded. "No rest for the weary," she muttered, a gallows attempt at humor that did nothing to lift her spirits.

She'd supervised the boys' studies, then read to them after their baths. Their mother demanded they be in bed and the lights out at nine. Maya was careful to comply. To fail was an invitation to wrath from Ms. Meredith.

Upon returning to her room, Maya had half expected Drake to be there, waiting for her. Finally, after almost an hour of fruitless study, she'd closed her textbook and prepared for bed. She should have known better. Coltons were a stubborn, unpredictable lot, and Drake was no exception.

She would live through this, she told her flagging

spirits. She'd lived through his leaving and finding that awful note, then realizing she was pregnant and telling her parents. What more could life throw at her?

Warily, she approached the door after tightening the belt to her robe. She opened it and peeked out.

"I want to talk to you," Drake announced in a low tone.

She considered locking the door. He probably knew how to unlock it without a key. The room had once been his before he struck out on his own.

Last summer, lying in bed with her, he'd told her of his childhood escapades, of sneaking in past curfew, of the hiding his father had once given him that had caused his mother to cry, making him feel so bad, he'd stopped skipping school and started studying. Now he slept in a room across the patio in the other wing of the house, a guest in his former home.

Surprised by an unexpected rush of sympathy, she moved back. He entered and closed the door.

His eyes, dark in the soft lamplight, as unyielding as a granite cliff, roamed over her. "Are you all right?" he asked quietly.

The question annoyed her. "Yes." Her answer seemed to stir his temper.

He scowled. "Only a fool would be out on a horse in your condition."

"The doctor said I could continue all my normal activities," she said, tilting her chin defiantly as resentment swept over her. "I always ride with the boys—"

"That was stupid. If you'd been thrown—" Drake

stopped, unable to block the image of her lying on the ground, hurt, dying.

"Damn you," he muttered. "If you can't think of yourself, think of the child. You're going to be a mother. You have an obligation to take care of the baby."

She moved away. "I know very well what my obligations are," she said coolly.

Then she walked over and sat in the old rocker that had been used to soothe many a Colton baby, including himself.

Drake stalked over to the desk chair, pulled it around and straddled it, his arms resting on the back while he observed the woman he'd returned home to see, the woman his father had mentioned in his last letter, telling Drake of Maya's pregnancy and suggesting that he come home.

An inner contraction, so strong it was painful, reminded Drake of last June and the week he'd spent at the ranch, home from his job with the Navy SEALs to celebrate his dad's sixtieth birthday.

What a memorable visit that had been. Someone had taken a potshot at his father. Shortly after that Drake had made love to the dark-haired Madonna who now watched him warily. "Inez says you're at least eight months along."

Her eyes widened. "You talked to my mother?"

"Yes. Since you refused to discuss it, I went to the one person I knew would tell me the truth. Why didn't you write?" he asked, changing tactics abruptly.

"Why didn't you?"

The challenge hit him right between the eyes. "I was off the beaten path most of the time."

The excuse sounded flimsy even to his ears. Her gaze flashed to him, then away, clearly expressing her disbelief.

He realized he'd grown up with this person, yet he didn't know her. He was three years older and had traveled the world; she'd spent her life here on the ranch. So why did she suddenly appear to be the one who was older and wiser?

Impending motherhood had changed her. It was more than the fact that her breasts were fuller and her tummy rounded. He sensed a primordial knowledge within her that hadn't been in the innocent young woman he'd loved, then left.

"My mission was dangerous," he tried to explain. "I move around. There's no future…I told you in the note I left."

"I believed you."

The simplicity of those three words threatened his self-control. They spoke of trust once given and now lost. Despair opened like a pit leading straight to the hell within him.

He exhaled heavily. He'd lived with the darkness for a long time. It was an old enemy, one he knew well. Standing, he thrust his hands into his pockets and paced to the window and back. "The child changes things."

"It isn't yours."

He stopped in front of her, not quite certain he'd heard right. She stood and faced him with that calm, older-than-time composure she'd recently acquired.

"It isn't your child," she repeated the denial.

The silence buzzed around them like an angry swarm of killer bees. She returned his hard stare without blinking, then she smiled slightly, not in amusement but as if the whole situation was one of supreme irony.

This distant, world-weary attitude baffled him more than her not bothering to write and tell him the news. He considered the conversation with her mother and remembered a name. "Then it's Andy Martin's?"

"Is that what my mother said?"

"Yes."

She tilted her chin in that stubborn way she had. "It's my baby. Mine and no one else's."

He'd been in enough standoffs with desperate people to know an impasse when he hit one. "Right. A virgin birth," he scoffed. "Look, this isn't getting us anywhere. I came home to find out the truth. I mean to know it before I leave."

"How did—" She clamped her lips together.

"How did I know about the baby? My father wrote. He said you were pregnant and that I should come home and get my affairs in order."

"Affairs," she repeated. "That's the operative word with you Coltons, isn't it?"

At that moment, he could have wrung her neck...or kissed her until she stopped this charade she'd decided to act out and responded to his kisses as she had last summer. His body went hard in an instant. Last June she'd been all sweet fire and sexy innocence, as eager to explore him as he had been her.

"You know me better than that," he said, the words coming out husky, the hunger evident.

Her hand flew to the neckline of the robe, which she pulled tightly closed as if fearing he might rip it from her lush body in a fit of uncontrollable passion.

"Do I? Maybe we don't know each other at all anymore," she suggested.

The sudden bleakness in her eyes struck a tender place under his breastbone. He thought of the woman who had told him her plans to finish her degree and teach school in Prosperino, or maybe start her own business and work with the troubled kids over at the Hopechest Ranch where she tutored students in remedial reading. It was her optimistic vision of the future that had forced him to write that note. It was a future he couldn't hope to share.

Abruptly he headed for the door. "You're right. Maybe we don't know each other now, but once we did. Your mother said I shouldn't upset you, but don't think this is the last of this conversation." He left quietly and headed outside for the steps that led down to the shore.

Maya rubbed her back and paced restlessly about the small room. Was her back hurting worse? Had she injured herself during the ride? She bit her lip against the pain and loneliness of the midnight hour. And the hunger that ate at her since she'd felt Drake's arms around her once more, strong and sure and capable.

How long before she forgot those moments last summer? Months? Years? A lifetime?

Unable to sleep lately or to sit for long periods, she walked the floor for hours. Most of the time she was confident of her ability to care for herself and a child, but sometimes, like now, her courage faltered.

Drake was a complication she hadn't foreseen. After his leaving last summer, with only a note to explain that they had no future, she hadn't thought he would even care if she was carrying his child.

The pain of that moment rushed over her anew, nearly causing her to cry out. She gritted her teeth and waited for it to pass. She'd learned, during the past eight months, that one could endure.

Sitting in the rocker and leaning forward as far as she could to relieve the pressure on her lower back, she knew she would have to admit the truth.

Unless there was a way to hide the truth...

She picked up the phone and dialed a number in L.A. When her sister answered, Maya spoke quickly and in a low voice.

"Lana, this is Maya. I have a question for you. Are you alone? Can you talk?"

"Well, hello, baby sister," Lana said in surprise. "Yes, I've just given my patient her final medication and was heading for bed. What's happening?"

Maya took a careful breath. "Drake Colton is home. His father told him about...about..."

"The baby?" Lana finished helpfully when Maya faltered.

"Yes. Listen, I know a DNA test would reveal the identity of the father, but no one could do anything to the baby without my consent, could they? Like take blood?"

"Is Drake threatening to take the baby from you?" Lana demanded indignantly.

"No, no, nothing like that. He doesn't know he's the father—I haven't told anyone but you—but he thinks he could be."

"Could be!" Lana's tone was shocked and angry. "How many affairs does he think you carry on at one time?"

"Never mind that. What about the DNA test?"

"I'm a private duty nurse, not a lawyer, but I think he could. I mean, a court order would do it."

"And the Coltons can afford the best lawyers in the world," Maya said, then sighed. She felt physically and emotionally exhausted.

She waited patiently as Lana tried to reassure her on her maternal rights, then said good-night.

The future seemed dark and even more uncertain all at once. How could she have been so foolish? she'd asked herself a thousand times during the intervening months.

She knew the answer. Love. The stuff of dreams.

Well, she was awake now, she mused ruefully, forcing a smile at her once idealistic self. Reality was a backache and an inability to find a sleeping position that her body accepted. Reality was also Drake Colton.

Unlike her longtime friend Andy Martin, Drake hadn't mentioned marriage. If she told him the baby was his, what would he do—insist on marriage or simply offer to support the child...or try to take it from her?

She had no idea what "putting his affairs in order"

meant to him. She again fought the despair that darkened her spirits at unguarded moments. She had known Drake all her life, but she truly hadn't a clue about his intentions.

Sighing, she got up and paced some more.

CHAPTER ONE

TWO

Drake hunched his shoulders against the chill and thrust his hands into his jeans pockets. The wind off the ocean had calmed, so the night wasn't as cold as expected.

He stalked along the rough shore, occasionally stumbling over a large rock mixed with the coarse sand and rounded pebbles of the beach. The moon cast a feeble light on the land, but it was instinct that led him to an alcove hidden among the boulders at the base of the cliff.

Folding his legs under him, he settled on a rise of sand that formed a bench under the rocky indentation and buried his face in his hands. He and his siblings had played at being pirates and sea captains in this alcove. He'd made love to Maya here.

Darkness overtook him, that desperation of the soul

that had been his companion for most of his life. Since his twin had died under the wheels of a car.

A shudder ran through him, as hot and painful as the bullet that had sliced through his hip.

"Drake, we're not supposed to go out on the highway," Michael called.

Drake pedaled his bike up the hill that overlooked the main road. "Come on. Let's go look for arrowheads on the other side of the road where the creek cuts through."

"Dad will kill us if he finds out."

"So how's he to know? I'm not going to tell. Come on, chicken. We won't be long."

His dad hadn't had to lay a hand on them. Michael, riding behind him, hadn't seen the car come speeding around the curve. Drake had. He'd yelled and run off the side of the road. Michael had been watching him, puzzled, right up until an instant before he'd been hit.

Drake groaned and lifted his head. He watched the turbulent roll of the waves onto the shore, each one a reminder of the past. His father had told him Michael's death wasn't his fault. The child psychologist his father had called in had said the same.

Drake's adult reasoning assured him this was true in the sense that he hadn't meant harm. But in his heart... In his heart, he would forever be calling for his brother to "Watch out" and knowing, even as he did, it was too late.

Shaking his head, he wondered why, with all his other worries, this one had come back to haunt him now.

Abruptly he pushed to his feet, needing movement

to dispel the memories of a past too powerful to forget.

Back at the house, he paused on the patio before going to his room. The light still shone in Maya's window. A shadow moved across the drawn shade.

Why was she still up?

He saw her stop and bend forward. She was in obvious pain. Panic shot through him. He rushed to her door and entered without knocking.

"Are you all right? Is the baby coming?" he demanded.

She brought herself up straight and stared at him as if he were out of his mind. "No. Go away."

Pushing a lock of hair behind her ear, she moved away from him, her hands on her back. Insight came to him. "Your back's hurting."

She sighed and didn't answer.

"Stay here," he advised as if she might disappear into the night. "I'll be right back."

Maya turned as quickly as she could, intending to tell him to leave her alone now and forever, but she faced only the door. He was already gone.

Glancing at the clock, she knew she had to get some rest. She slipped out of the robe, got in bed and turned out the light. Lying on her side with a knee drawn up to support her midsection, she firmly closed her eyes.

She'd counted three hundred sheep when the door opened and the light was switched on again. "What is it?" she snapped.

"Liniment," Drake said in a tone that implied this explained everything. "Stay still. I'll rub your back."

Shock rolled over her. "You'll do no such thing!"

She'd die before she let him see her in her nightgown, her stomach round as a roly-poly.

He snatched the covers down and sat on the edge of the bed. "This will help you sleep," he assured her, as if that was the only concern about him being in her room at...

"It's almost one in the morning," she said.

"Yeah. You need your rest."

He pushed her gently down on the bed, then opened the bottle. The pungent scent of horse liniment filled the room. With one hand, he pulled the straps of her gown off her shoulders and down her arms.

"Slip this down to your waist—"

"No!" Panic was beginning to muddle her thoughts. She was entirely too aware of his warmth next to her hip and of the hour and of the yearning, the remembered hunger, that flooded her from deep within.

Pushing upward, she realized that was a mistake as her gown slipped off her breasts. She threw her arms over her chest and huddled against the sheet as liquid heat ran in her blood.

"That's better," Drake said.

She heard the slosh of the liniment, then felt his hand on her bare shoulders, accompanied by the strong smell and cooling effects of horse medicine. Realizing he wouldn't leave until he'd accomplished his task, she lay stiffly and let him rub her neck and down her spine to the edge of the nightgown.

When his fingers slipped under the material, every nerve in her body jerked.

"Easy," he murmured, his voice low and sexy, soft the way it had been when they made love, endlessly tender as he coaxed her into wild passion.

Relentlessly, he continued, rubbing and rubbing, pushing the gown down as he went lower until it finally rested at her waist. Using both hands, he massaged deeply on either side of her backbone and into the small of her back. It was painful, yet perversely made her feel better. Her eyes closed of their own accord as the pain receded.

She groaned with relief as strained muscles slowly relaxed for the first time in weeks. He shifted closer, putting one knee up on the bed to rest by her side.

"That's better," he murmured.

Minutes went by in silence, broken only when he wet his hands with the liniment before starting his massage again.

His fingers were magic. The stiffness melted away, replaced by a languid uneasiness that also faded as his touch became gentler. Now he rubbed soothingly.

Exhaling on a deep sigh, she slipped into slumber with no dreams to haunt her rest.

Drake continued rubbing lightly, not quite ready to stop touching her. Her skin was as smooth and soft as he remembered. Her warmth reached down inside him to that place of piercing cold that had been with him almost as long as he could remember. Only Maya had ever eased it.

He screwed the cap on the liniment bottle and placed it on the night table, then turned out the lamp.

The moonlight fell in an oblong of brilliance on the carpet. He couldn't keep the thought from his mind that next door, Teddy slept in the bed that had once belonged to his twin.

Last summer, lying in this bed, he'd told Maya about the accident and his part in it, about the guilt he sometimes felt for being alive. She'd simply held him closer and had made tender love to him until he'd forgotten the past. He grimaced slightly. They'd both forgotten everything, including the need to use protection, during those hazy moments of delight.

It had never occurred to him that she would become pregnant. He'd never thought of having children.

Without considering the act, he ran his hand around her waist and rested it on the hard mound of her abdomen. To his amazement, he felt something press against his palm, then he experienced a series of bumps. A funny feeling washed over him as he realized the baby was kicking the spot where his hand rested. It came to him that the child was alive and well and *real*.

Very real.

Maybe it was sheer vanity, but he knew it was his. It seemed to him that the baby knew him, too, that it was welcoming him home.

About time.

He started as the words popped into his head as if his son or daughter were speaking to him through mental telepathy.

"Yeah, I know," he said softly. "Now if we could

get your mother to admit the truth, maybe we could figure out where to go from here.''

Maya shifted in her sleep and gave a little moan. She sighed and became still once more, her knee drawn up on the mattress to support the weight of the baby. Feeling an odd constriction in his chest, he stood.

Carefully he lifted the straps of her gown back into place, then covered her. After a last long look filled with needs he couldn't deny, he rose and slipped out of the room.

In his own bed, he tried to think of a plan of action. That was why his missions were usually a success. He thought of every contingency and had a solution for each and every one. He'd do the same with Maya. As soon as he figured out what her problem was, other than anger at him.

Maya got the boys up and off to school as usual. Life did go on, or else Ms. Meredith would have a fit.

Hearing the vacuum going in the living room, she knew her mother was in there. The sprawling hacienda-style home was vacuumed and dusted twice a week. In the spring and fall, it underwent a cleaning that literally left no bed unturned. The same thing happened in the Ramirez household.

Maya crept into the kitchen. Sure enough, it was empty for the moment, although she could smell a roast in the oven and traces of the bacon from breakfast. Not hungry, but thinking of the baby, she prepared two pieces of toast and poured a glass of milk.

She set them, along with a mug of coffee, on the table.

Halfway through the meal, Drake ambled in from outside. He looked devilishly handsome in old jeans and boots, a blue shirt and denim jacket. He brought the scent of the outdoors and horses into the room with him. After getting a mug of coffee, he joined her at the table. There, she got a whiff of his cologne.

It transported her back in time to days of riding and playing with the two younger boys at their heels while they searched for arrowheads and wild berries. To long walks along the beach while they talked their hearts out. To nights—

With a sharp intake of breath, she pulled herself back from that abyss. Remembering brought nothing but pain and the cold light of day to the dreams she'd harbored.

"What is it?" he immediately wanted to know.

She glanced at him. A mistake. His golden gaze held hers for a long, serious minute and asked questions she couldn't answer. She looked away. "Nothing."

But the longing was already in her. She wanted him to sweep her into his arms and make everything okay. She wanted him to wipe out the last eight months of worry and embarrassment, of startled and disapproving glances as her family and friends realized she was expecting. She wanted things that weren't going to happen.

With a stoic smile, she wondered who she thought she—the housekeeper's daughter—was, to set her sights upon a son of the mighty Colton clan.

"Share," he requested.

She shook her head. "Just musing on the ironies of life." She took a sip of coffee, then washed down her vitamins with the last gulp of milk.

Her maternity top fluttered as the baby moved. Maya waited. Sometimes the movements were too vigorous for comfort. Then she would have to sit for a few minutes and wait for the baby to settle down before she could go on.

"Is the baby moving?" Drake asked, leaning closer and peering at her abdomen.

"Yes."

He wasn't put off by her abrupt answer. "May I?" he asked and, without waiting, laid his hand on her tummy.

Maya was immediately aware of heat rushing to the spot, as if a sun had suddenly blazed to life in her.

"It kicked my hand last night," Drake said.

"Wh-what?"

"After you went to sleep, I touched you like this. The baby kicked against my hand several times."

He grinned, his even teeth a white slash in his tanned face, making him startlingly handsome, the way Tom Cruise was when he flashed his million-watt smile. It was enough to make women fall at their feet, both the actor and this man.

Chalk it up to being human, she advised her smarting heart. She'd had a crush on Drake Colton most of her life. Once, at seventeen, she'd thought he was interested in her when he came home from college, but he'd abruptly withdrawn, avoiding her the rest of his stay.

It had hurt, but she'd gotten past the dreams she'd spun of them at that time. She would again. It was merely a wee bit more complicated this time around.

Removing his hand, she said politely, "Please don't."

He leaned back in his chair, steam rising from the coffee as he drank deeply, his eyes never leaving her. When he set the cup down, he asked, "Do you know whether it's a boy or a girl?"

The silence grew too long to be comfortable.

She had to clear her throat before speaking. "A girl," she said in a near whisper. She cleared her throat again. "I had a sonogram. It's a girl."

He nodded solemnly, and she couldn't tell whether he was pleased or not.

Really, she had to stop thinking this way, as if he might be delighted at the prospect of their having a child. Those hopes belonged to her younger, more idealistic self. Drake's note had made it clear his intentions had not extended to a future, not with her at any rate.

"Did you get a picture of her?"

She nodded.

"Maybe you'll let me see it sometime," he suggested softly, almost wistfully. "Have you picked a name yet?"

Her chest tightened. "Marissa. Marissa Ramirez."

His face hardened for a fraction of a second, then the expression was gone. He smiled as he considered the name. "Marissa. I like that. If she's lucky, she'll be as beautiful as her mother."

His eyes glided over her in a visual caress, warm and exciting and promising more than he ever meant to give. Maya set her mug down abruptly as her hand trembled wildly, threatening to spill hot liquid down her front.

"I have studying to do." She rose, refilled her cup and retreated to the relative safety of her room. She stayed there until lunch.

Hearing the others congregating in the dining room and kitchen, she knew she had to make an appearance. If she didn't, her mother would come to check on her, worry on her brow as she fretted about lack of appetite and its effects on the baby. There would be no retreat from harsh reality at the present.

Maya squared her shoulders and walked down the hall, ready for the firing squad, so to speak. Drake wasn't in the kitchen. Relieved, she turned to her mother. "Can I help?"

Inez nodded distractedly. She dumped a stack of homemade tortillas into a cloth-lined basket. "Take these to the dining room," she said. "Check if there's enough salsa on the table."

Maya's heart dropped straight to her toes, but pride wouldn't allow her to refuse. After all, she had opened her mouth and volunteered. Another lesson in life from the school of hard knocks, she reminded herself, trying for humor to bolster her flagging courage.

"Oh, and butter," her mother added, stirring a pot

and tasting the contents before adding more seasoning.

Maya put fresh butter on a crystal dish, picked up the basket and went into the formal dining room. Maybe none of the family had gathered yet.

As if she would have such good fortune.

It was worse than she imagined. Drake and his father were at the table, deep in conversation, when she walked in. There was a beat of silence, then Joe rose with a smile.

"Maya, you're looking beautiful today." He glanced at his son. "There's something about an expectant mother, isn't there? A glow that's special."

"Yes." Drake's voice was low, sexy.

Maya felt the blush start at her toes and work its way up. By the time it reached her hairline, she felt like a fresh-boiled lobster.

"Didn't mean to embarrass you," Joe murmured, his gaze so full of delight and kindness, she could have wept.

"No, it's all right," she managed to say past the lump in her throat.

When she dared look at Drake, his gaze was non-committal, with no emotion that she could detect. "Mom sent some tortillas and butter." She placed them on the table near the men.

After checking the salsa dish, she hurried back to the kitchen. "Here," Inez said, thrusting a platter into Maya's hands. "Take these. The new helper I hired didn't show up. I have to get the rest of the food ready."

Maya suppressed a twinge of guilt. Had it not been

for Drake, she would have been giving her mom a hand. Instead, she'd hid in her room all morning. And accomplished nothing in the way of studying. She had a big test coming up later in the month.

She took the huge platter of burritos to the dining room table. Mexican food was one of Joe's favorite meals and in spite of Ms. Meredith, her mother served it often.

Maya returned to the kitchen for bowls of refried beans and Spanish rice. In the dining room, after checking the table to make sure she hadn't missed anything, she again turned toward the kitchen, aware of a brooding gaze on her each time she'd entered the room.

"Why don't you join us?" Joe asked.

Her feet took root and she couldn't move. She shook her head and felt her hair swish against her face. Realizing she was overreacting, she managed a smile and tried to decline politely, but it was useless. Drake had already pulled a chair out for her. Joe took her arm and guided her into it.

"Well," she said with a strained smile, "since you insist."

Joe's smile was understanding and benign. She wasn't sure about Drake's. It held a more menacing quality.

"How are your studies going?" the older Colton asked, serving her the platter of burritos before taking two for himself.

"Fine, sir. I made the dean's list."

"As usual," Joe said in approval. He passed the plate to Drake.

The son, she noted, took four. How could his lean frame burn up so much food, she wondered, something she had asked once before.

"I think a lot," he'd answered at the time. He'd kissed her deeply. "And engage in vigorous activity," he'd added, then he'd proceeded to show her what he meant.

The heat surged to her face at the memory. She spooned out rice and beans, then passed the bowls to Joe, who sat at the end of the long table with Drake on his left, directly across from her so that she met his eyes every time she looked up.

Ms. Meredith breezed into the room, bringing the scent of expensive blended perfume. Without acknowledging Maya's presence, she wrinkled her nose at the food, then informed her husband she had a luncheon engagement in town and, without so much as a goodbye to her son, left.

Maya tried not to feel sorry for Drake and the other Colton children, but it was hard. Her own mother, Inez, loved kids and lavishly showed it. Other than periods of intense interest in her two youngest children, Drake's mother mostly ignored her children. It was a riddle because she hadn't always been that way.

From her childhood, Maya recalled Ms. Meredith as a gentle, laughing woman who would run and play with her children and husband as if she, too, were young and full of life.

Glancing up, she saw Drake's eyes follow his mother as she left the house.

Maya suddenly sensed the need of the boy for the comfort his mother would have once given him. Then his gaze hardened and he was a man again, tough, resilient and determined, the kind of man the Navy called on for its most dangerous missions.

It was a life he relished. As if he courted death. As if he dared it to come close.

She ate quickly, sorrow in her heart. Maybe Drake didn't know it, but there was something in him...not exactly a death wish—nothing so drastic as that—but a core of darkness nevertheless, one that he had never come to grips with.

"I wanted to ask you about the Hopechest Ranch," Joe continued after the brief interruption. "I want your opinion. Do you think it's helping the children?"

"Oh, yes. It's a wonderful place and has a fine reputation. The reading program is excellent. In my opinion," she added, realizing she might have sounded arrogant.

"I'm thinking of increasing the endowment this year."

"That would be good, sir. The courts are referring more children there than the school can take."

"Mmm." The older man thought a bit. "Drake, while you're home, maybe you can take a tour of the Hopechest and recommend something more we can do—a new stable or arena, perhaps? Or an additional bunkhouse."

"I'll look into it," Drake promised.

"Good. That's good, son."

Maya was touched by the obvious pride and trust the elder Colton placed in his son. Drake needed to see he was appreciated for himself.

Abruptly, she cut off the thought. Drake didn't need her concern and pity. He was a grown man. She'd do well to keep out of other people's business, especially when her own emotions were totally unreliable at this point.

Remember that advice, she mocked her soft heart, and you'll get along a lot better in the world. Except she was going to love her child devotedly and show that love just as her parents had done with her and her sister, Lana.

She sighed in resignation. Yeah, she was one tough cookie.

"How are you feeling this morning?" Drake asked, looking directly at her.

His father turned his kind gaze on her, too, while they waited for an answer.

"Fine," she murmured. "I'm just fine."

"Back not hurting?"

The question sounded so intimate, she felt as if he were making love to her right there at the table. The awful blush started again. "No. Excuse me. I have to be at the Hopechest soon." She picked up her plate of half-eaten food and fled.

"You didn't eat much," her mother noted as soon as Maya entered the kitchen.

"I had plenty. I have to run now, Mom." She kissed her mother's cheek. "Love you."

"Love you," Inez repeated, her dark eyes checking her over anxiously.

On the drive to the children's ranch, Maya wished she didn't have to hurt her parents. They loved her and worried about her, but she just couldn't admit

Drake was the father of her child and that he didn't want them.

The contents of that note still burned in her heart, making her chest tighten so that she could scarcely breathe whenever she recalled it. His lovemaking had meant nothing. He'd made no promises, not one.

Pushing her troubles into the background, she turned in at the Hopechest Ranch. The kids who lived here had it rough. Compared to them, her life was a piece of cake.

"Hey, Miss Ramirez," Johnny Collins called, spotting her getting out of her car. He came over to help carry her books and papers.

"Hey, Johnny," she greeted the fourteen-year-old, one of her favorites. His mother had abandoned him and his father years ago. The boy's father had taken to drinking and couldn't keep a job. Johnny had been caught with his hand in the till, so to speak, at a fast-food place where he'd lied about his age and gotten a job. "Did you get through the book I assigned last week?"

"Yeah. I wrote down the words I didn't know and looked them up after I got through each chapter, like you said. It made reading easier."

"Good." They went into the classroom where she privately tutored the kids who were way behind. "I got your test graded. You aced it. Wow!" she exclaimed softly, giving him the praise he deserved.

His dark eyes lit up. She noted the golden flecks in them and thought of Drake's dark eyes that flashed golden when the light hit them.

"Okay, let's see your list of words," she requested when she was at her desk and ready to start.

For the next two hours she worked with Johnny, then a group of students who were further advanced. At three, she rushed home to check on Joe Junior and Teddy and make sure they did their homework correctly. Ms. Meredith was a stickler about that, too.

Drake was in the corral, working with one of the young cow ponies when she arrived. She stood by the car and watched him for a few minutes.

He had a firm touch on the reins and made sure the gelding knew what was expected and performed the task correctly before he went on to something else. He would make a good teacher for the students at the children's ranch—

Reality check, she interrupted herself. Drake didn't need her advice on what to do with his life when he grew tired of risking it on daring rescues in places where he could get himself shot on sight. It wasn't her business.

Just as she turned to head inside, Drake stopped his mount beside the fence. He dipped his head toward her in greeting, then simply watched her, making her think of lunch and the way he had looked at her then. There was an invitation in those dark depths, but she didn't know what it was an invitation to.

The baby stirred and kicked vigorously as if sensing her agitation. Flustered, she rushed into the house.

Three

"Maya, come with us," Joe Junior shouted as soon as she stepped in the door. "Drake's gonna teach us how to rope."

"Yeah, we'll be rodeo champions someday!" Teddy said.

"Indoor voices, please," Maya reminded them, going into her room and storing her book bag before swapping her flats for sneakers. "What about your homework?"

The boys vowed they'd do it before dinner and give up their hour of television if need be.

"Okay."

"We can?" Joe looked disbelieving, then he let out a whoop, quickly suppressed. He and Teddy took off.

Maya's heart did a somersault. Drake was good to his younger brothers. He obviously cared for them.

They needed love and approbation from someone other than her. Their mother was too unpredictable in her love.

Their father loved them, but there was a sadness in him that Maya thought the youngsters sensed, so they tended to be subdued around him. Besides, Joe was deeply involved with all the other problems in the Coltons' lives at present—the shootings, the disappearance of Emily.

With Drake, the boys could do "guy" things. The shared companionship was good for all of them, Drake included. The boys touched a soft spot in him. He needed that.

Not that she was concerned with his needs, she reminded herself. Pulling on a jacket, she headed outside to keep an eye on her two charges. Ms. Meredith had made it very plain that she paid Maya to be with the boys and keep them from harm. That meant keeping them within view at all times.

Arriving at the paddock, Maya found Drake had set up two sawhorses with brooms for heads and was showing the boys how to hold their lariats. She couldn't help but laugh. He turned his intense gaze on her with a quickness that dried up the merriment.

"Your laughter makes the day brighter," he said.

Maya was aware of the boys looking from one to the other, then at each other. They giggled in the way kids do when grown-ups say funny things.

"Is this right?" Joe asked, directing his brother's attention to their concerns once more.

Leaning on the fence, Maya watched Drake start the two youngsters close to the sawhorses. Joe, being older, caught on quicker than Teddy. Drake moved him back to ten feet, then worked with Teddy until he got the hang of tossing the rope over the broom.

After an hour, Maya called out, "Ten more minutes, guys."

"Then what?" Drake asked.

He gave her a sexy once-over that startled her thoughts right out of her head. "Then it's time for homework," she said, gathering her wits.

When the boys protested, Drake shushed them. "You have to plan your time carefully to get everything done. That's what a good SEAL does. You've done roping, now it's time for the next item on the agenda, right, teacher?"

"Uh, right," she echoed.

"Vamoose!" Drake ordered, then grabbed a sawhorse in each hand and left the paddock.

Joe and Teddy climbed over the fence and dropped to the ground beside Maya. "Drake's really good," Joe told her. "He could be a rodeo champion if he wanted."

"Yeah. That's what I'm gonna be," Teddy decided.

Joe gave him a shove. "Ha!"

"I am!"

"Enough, guys. Don't argue. Discuss—that's the rule. And don't touch another person without permission. Joe, ten minutes earlier to bed."

"Aww," Joe started to complain.

Ms. Meredith opened the door and glared at all three of them. "You will lower your voices at once," she ordered.

"Yes, ma'am," both boys intoned simultaneously.

Maya felt like echoing the boys' subdued manner. She had stopped "ma'am-ing" Ms. Meredith a year ago upon realizing that, in order to be taken as an equal, she must act as one. She would not be subservient.

"Have the boys done their homework?" Meredith asked her with a severe frown.

"We're on our way to do that now. Drake was teaching them how to rope. It's excellent training for eye-hand coordination," she said in a firm teacher-knows-best voice.

She smiled with an assurance she was far from feeling and hoped she didn't get a dressing-down in front of her young charges. They tended to take her side, ending with all three of them getting a lecture.

To her relief, the other woman nodded and left them in the hall while she went into the living room to speak to her husband. Maya quickly herded the boys to her room where she set them to work on their lessons. She got out her own books and studied the physical, mental and emotional development of children from kindergarten to sixth grade.

Drake peeled out of his clothes, took a quick shower, dressed, then hurried to the kitchen. Maya wasn't there.

"Where...are the boys?" he amended his question.

Inez Ramirez, longtime housekeeper, friend and confidante to the Colton family, studied him for an uncomfortable five seconds before answering. "Maya took their dinner to her room. They aren't finished with their homework yet.''

Disappointment hit him. He tried to keep it from showing. Growing up, he and all the kids on the ranch had decided Inez could read minds. She always knew when they had done something they shouldn't as soon as they walked into the house. At the present moment, he felt as if she knew of each and every tryst he'd had with her daughter last summer…and of the lustful dreams he'd been having of Maya every night since then.

"Thanks," he said politely and headed for the living room where he'd seen his parents earlier. He paused when he got within earshot.

"You simply have to pay it. It's been months,'' Drake heard his father say.

"Really, Joe,'' Meredith said in obvious annoyance. "It's only a couple of thousand. You'd think I'd asked for your life savings.''

"Precisely why I did what I did with your credit cards. You have an allowance. I suggest you pay your bills with it.''

"But some of these charges were for your birthday party!''

Drake winced at his father's laughter. He'd never heard that tone before—cold and harsh and cynical.

"Not one of the family's better days,'' Joe Senior continued in the same vein.

"I…no, it wasn't,'' his mother agreed, her voice going soft. "It frightened me, that you might have been killed, or at the least, incapacitated.''

Drake waited for his father's reply, but heard nothing. In another second, he heard the tap of his mother's heels. He stayed in the dining room until she went down the hall toward her room. He heard her door shut with a brittle slam.

After another minute, he ventured into the other room. His father stood at the window, his face expressionless as he stared out at the deepening twilight. He turned when Drake entered, then smiled in greeting.

Drake felt a tightening in his chest. No matter what his father's disappointments or trials were in life, Joe always had time for children, whether his own or the foster kids that stayed with them at the ranch. Drake admired that quality in his sire and tried to emulate it with his younger brothers.

"How are things with you?" Joe asked.

"Fine, sir," Drake began, then stopped. "Well, maybe not so good. I'm not making much headway with Maya."

Joe raised his eyebrows in question.

"She won't tell me who the father of the child is," Drake admitted.

"A brandy?" Joe asked, pouring one for himself.

"Please."

Drake accepted a snifter, then sat on the sofa after his father settled in a chair. The feel of leather, the shine of the furniture and faint scent of lemon oil were familiar and comforting.

His father swirled the brandy in his glass, then fastened a piercing gaze on him. "Does that matter?"

Drake was startled by the question. "Well, yes,"

he began. "That is… If it's mine, then naturally I'll do the right thing."

"What if it isn't?" Joe persisted. "Joe Junior was left on our doorstep. Your mother and I adopted him and raised him as if he were our own flesh and blood."

Drake nodded. It was such ancient history, he'd truly forgotten that little Joe was a foundling.

"If Maya's child couldn't be yours, I assume you would have said so and not come home."

Drake met his father's level gaze. "It could be. I think…actually, I'm sure it is. But she won't say so," he finished in frustration.

"Have you asked her to marry you?"

Drake smiled in irony. "We haven't gotten that far."

"I take it that you don't want the marriage?" Joe questioned dryly.

Drake fought the storm of emotion that rushed through him. "I didn't plan on having a wife and family. My life is uncertain at best."

"And extremely dangerous the rest of the time," Joe concluded. "Yet women and children do manage when husbands and fathers have tough jobs that take them away from home for long periods. It's all in how the family handles it. Love makes a big difference."

Drake knew his father was questioning his feelings for Maya. He stared out the window at the dark shadows cast by a tree swaying in the night wind. The darker shadows in his soul shifted painfully. Maya was like the sun. She was all the bright, good things in life, the things forever out of his reach.

"Dinner," Inez called softly from the dining room.

Joe observed the flicker of emotion pass through his son's eyes. Drake was a man, with a man's needs. Sex was part of that, but so was love. A life without it was desolate indeed.

Suppressing a sigh, he rose and led the way into the dining room where the family was gathering for the evening meal. It should have been a joyous time of the day.

He sat at the head of the table, Drake at his left. River and Sophie, now married and expecting—his and Meredith's first grandchild!—joined them. Their new house which River had designed and built himself, was a beauty, but Joe loved when they visited the main house.

Meredith entered, nodded graciously when the children greeted her, and took her place.

Glancing at Drake, Joe thought of young Teddy. He'd had an impulse to confide to his older son that the youngest Colton wasn't his but he loved the boy as if he were.

That fact wasn't something a man could tell his child. However Meredith had changed, she was still the mother of their children. That she adored Joe Junior and Teddy, Joe couldn't deny.

A sadness reaching clear to the depths of his soul rolled over him. Drake was struggling to realize just what his relationship was with Maya, but Joe had had no doubts the first time he'd met Meredith. Neither had she. They had known they were in love from the first.

Where had it all gone?

* * *

Maya was relieved when she walked out of the doctor's office. She and little Marissa were doing fine. Her wild ride hadn't harmed the baby, thank goodness. She backed out of the busy parking lot next to the medical building and nearly ran over Peggy Honeywell who ran the bed-and-breakfast, Honeywell House, in Prosperino.

They grinned and waved at each other. When the coast was clear, Maya ran a few errands and drove carefully to the high school. She met Andy Martin in his classroom.

"How's it going?" he greeted her cheerfully, his eyes sweeping over her blossoming figure as if to check her progress.

Just the way every person she met looked her over nowadays. She sometimes felt like a beached whale with a curious crowd milling around, trying to figure out what to do with her.

"Great," she assured him. She got out some test papers. "Here are Johnny's latest exams. I really appreciate your looking them over for me. He needs more help in math than I can spare him, I'm afraid."

Andy studied the papers and made some notes in the margins beside the wrong answers. "Mm," he said once in a while. "Ah, yes."

Maya thought his comments sounded promising. The boy was smart, precocious in the way of many children who'd had to raise themselves, but he was sadly lacking in basic skills such as reading and arithmetic.

"Okay, I think I can come up with a program of

study for him that will bring him up to par." Andy squinted and gave her an assessing look.

"What?" she asked.

"How about I come out to the ranch Saturday morning? Could you fit that into your schedule? I'd like to work out some word problems, then check with you on his vocabulary level. We'll see how well he does on reading comprehension when it relates to problem solving."

"That would be perfect. Thanks, Andy. You have no idea what a load this is off my mind. I think Johnny has college potential, but he's going to need extra help to get him up to speed."

"No problem." He checked his watch. "You feel like an early supper or maybe a snack?"

When she'd realized she was pregnant with Drake's child, she'd broken off entirely with Andy, refusing even the most casual of meetings with him. When he'd learned of the child, he'd sought her out and offered marriage.

No questions asked.

Not like Drake, who apparently wanted to know exactly when she'd became pregnant and with whom. She would never forgive him for that, no matter how sorry she might feel for him because of his parents' problems or his sad past.

"I think not."

"I hear Drake Colton is back in town," Andy murmured, a speculative note in his voice.

She stared at the chalkboard, unable to totally lie and unwilling to admit she'd been a fool. "Yes, he's home for...for a vacation, I suppose."

"Maya—"

She jumped to her feet—well, okay, it was more of a lunge—and smiled brightly. "I really have to go. The boys are on their own and probably ignoring their homework."

Andy walked out to the car with her. He opened the door, then lightly clasped her arm. "I've been your friend for a long time. You know that, don't you?"

She nodded unhappily. She'd never meant to hurt him.

"You can come to me at any time. To talk. To just get away. Whatever. Okay?"

"Thanks." Impulsively she kissed his cheek, then quickly got in the car and left before she bawled like a motherless calf right there on the main street of town. That would start a buzz on the old grapevine!

Andy watched, his eyes filled with kindness and worry, until she'd turned the corner and was out of sight.

Maya sniffed, sighed and turned her mind to her duties at the Colton estate. She had a paper to finish, then she had to e-mail it to the professor. That was after she supervised the boys and got them to bed.

Heavens, but she was tired. And her back hurt. Also her feet. For a second, she wondered how she'd gotten into such a situation.

"By being stupid," she muttered sarcastically. "By falling in love," she added on a sadder note as she parked near the house and pushed herself wearily out of the car.

She went from one task to another for the next few

hours, checking Joe's and Teddy's homework, helping her mother finish getting supper on the table, making sure the boys had their baths and were in bed at lights-out, then doing her own work. She saw Drake briefly in passing. He gave her a narrow-eyed scrutiny and barely spoke.

Okay, she could handle that, she assured herself as she slipped into a clean nightgown. After all, she'd handled that brief, shattering note—

A soft knock sounded on the door.

"Not tonight," she called out.

Drake opened the door.

"I'm really going to have to remember to lock the door from now on," she said in protest.

"Why? Are men lining up to get inside?"

She closed her eyes and spoke to the room at large. "Do I have to take these kinds of insults? No." She glared at Drake. "Please get out before I scream bloody murder."

He had the grace to look slightly remorseful. He paced the room, then took up his usual position straddling her desk chair. "I saw you in town today."

She frowned. "So?"

He slapped his hand on the back of the chair. "Dammit, you were with another man, kissing him right out on the street. What gives?"

Maya stared blankly at Drake. "I haven't the foggiest idea what you mean."

"Are you with him?" When she continued to stare at him, he added, "Is it serious between you two?"

She realized who he meant. "Andy is my friend."

"That was Andy Martin?" He frowned. "He's changed."

"Well, that's because you probably haven't seen him since high school. People do grow up. Some people," she tossed in for good measure.

"Meaning I haven't?" He laughed softly, cynically, at that ridiculous accusation.

The baby did a double flip, and Maya grimaced and pressed her side in discomfort. Would she ever make it to her due date? At this moment, she had her doubts.

"I'll get the liniment," Drake volunteered.

"No—"

But as usual, he was quicker than a cat. He retrieved the bottle from the table and opened it. Then he chuckled.

"What's so funny?" she demanded, feeling big and clumsy and at the end of her tether.

"Our daughter is going to think her parents are of the equine variety if we keep using the horse liniment to rub you down."

"She wouldn't if you'd just leave me alone."

"I can't," he stated, so simply she couldn't think of an argument to convince him he could. "Lie down," he requested, gesturing toward the bed.

Sighing, she heaved herself up and went to the bed, not caring if he saw her as round as a pumpkin in her gown. It wasn't as if he were going to ravish her.

Memories rushed at her, tilting her already shaky emotions. Tears sprang to her eyes. Eight months ago, he had laved her with kisses and caresses and sweet, sweet words of love. And then he'd left.

"What is it?" he asked softly.

She shook her head. Maybe the words hadn't been those of love, only need and physical hunger. Except she'd felt the love in him, saw it in his eyes. Or thought she had. "Nothing. It's nothing."

Putting a knee on the bed, she let herself down on the cool sheet and turned on her stomach as much as she could, her leg drawn up to take her weight. She sighed at her own awkwardness, then at her foolish dreams.

With the same mastery he'd shown last night, Drake massaged the pain away, then rubbed her lightly until the tension also dissolved. She sank toward slumber.

"You're beautiful," he murmured at one point.

"If you like whales."

Laughing softly, he set the liniment bottle on the table, then slid both hands over her plump waist. "Let me touch you. Turn toward me. Please."

The request was so humble, she couldn't refuse. She rolled to her back with his help. He ran his hands over her abdomen in gentle forays, a look of intense concentration on his face.

"A child is such a miracle, isn't it?" he said softly at one point when the baby kicked against his hand.

"Yes." She hardly dared speak aloud, the moment seemed so fragile. Longing coursed through her. Life could be so wonderful, if he loved her, if he truly wanted her and the baby.

"I can't believe we created this. I never thought about having a child."

She remained silent in the face of his seeming enchantment. Her heart fluttered in agitation, not sure what the moment meant, or where it was leading.

His eyes met her questioning ones. A tender smile lit his handsome face, warming her and soothing the agitation. Silently they shared the magic of creation as he continued to caress her through the silky material of her gown.

She would remember this forever.

The saltiness of tears stung her eyes and she closed them so Drake wouldn't see.

"Maya," he said thoughtfully after a while, "we'd better marry soon. Before the baby gets here."

As far as proposals went, she would rate it around a one out of a possible ten. Angry with herself for falling under his spell again, she pushed away from the gentleness of his touch.

"Why would we do that?" she asked, striving to sound calm and reasonable. "The baby is my responsibility, not yours. You needn't concern yourself about us."

Instead of answering angrily as she'd expected, he merely watched her from those dark eyes with their golden glints that reminded her of a wild creature at times.

"I am concerned," he finally told her. "We created this life together—"

"No," she said.

His chest lifted and fell as he took a deep breath, then let it out. "What would a DNA test disclose?"

Her gaze dropped before his probing one. "I won't marry in order to give the baby a name. Ramirez is a respectable family name, one I'm proud of."

"And so you should be. Your parents are two of the finest people I know. However, that doesn't solve the question of *this* baby. Our baby," he added softly, his hands sweeping over her again.

"It's my problem. I'll take responsibility for it."

This time the anger showed in his eyes. His expression became grim. "Do you think so little of me that you would deny me my own flesh and blood? Or my part in what happened between us?"

"I—I don't know," she said, torn between dreams and reality.

He went absolutely still, staring at her in disbelief. She knew then that she'd wounded him.

"I'm sorry. I didn't mean... It's just that I want the best for the baby. A forced marriage doesn't seem to be the answer."

"I'd go willingly to the altar."

His quick assurance didn't ease her heart. She wouldn't accept marriage because of his strong sense of duty. While he might love the child, he would hate her for tying him to a union he didn't want.

"Your note said there was no place in your life for a wife," she reminded him.

"A man says some damn fool things under stress. I'm sorry for leaving the way I did. I'd gotten an emergency call and had to return to duty. I should have told you instead of ducking out while you were asleep. That was a stupid, cowardly thing to do."

He sounded so sincere, she didn't know what to say. No retort came to mind, yet she couldn't let herself feel sorry for him. When she sighed, it came out shaky and uncertain.

His face softened. He turned the light out, then leaned over her. "We're not through yet. Before I leave, you'll tell me everything I want to know. We'll get through this and get it resolved."

They watched each other for another long minute in the dim glow from moonlight. She sensed desolation in him, this man of depth and darkness who came to her from a sense of duty. At that moment, she knew what she wanted from him.

Love, of course, but more than that, she wanted joy from him. She wanted him to be happy in their love. But the shadows within were stronger than his feelings, whatever they were, for her and their child.

He touched her eyes gently. "Sleep."

In another second he was gone. She felt the emptiness in the room and deep inside, at that place where hurt collected into a hard ball of longing.

The baby was quiet, as if she felt it, too.

Four

————

Wednesday morning, Joe Colton answered the doorbell himself instead of waiting for Inez to emerge from wherever she was working in the house. Thaddeus Law, the local police detective assigned to the Colton shooting stood there, looking grim.

Reacting from gut instinct, Joe steeled himself for bad news. "Come in," he said and led the way into his study. "Coffee?" he asked the lawman, who was in his mid-thirties but looked older, as if he'd led a hard life.

Losing his wife in an airplane crash and trying to raise a preschooler on his own had probably contributed a few worry lines to the man's face. However, Thaddeus had recently wed Heather McGrath, Joe's personal assistant and daughter of Peter McGrath,

Joe's foster brother, so presumably the detective now lived a happier life.

"That would be good," Thaddeus replied, removing his hat and placing it on his knee as he took the chair Joe indicated. "It's drizzly and chilly again, a day to stay inside before a fire."

He nodded toward the fireplace where a blaze crackled merrily, dispelling the dampness of the morning.

"Yes, another cold front moved in last night." Joe poured coffee from an insulated carafe into two mugs, then added a third when he saw Drake at the door. "Come on in, son. You know Thaddeus, don't you?"

"Of course." Drake entered and shook hands with the detective before taking the coffee cup. He settled in a chair next to Thaddeus, his gaze intelligent and alert. Joe's heart warmed with pride and love.

"Do you have any news?" Drake asked the lawman.

"Yes." Thaddeus turned to Joe. "Is your wife available?"

Joe wasn't surprised that Meredith's presence was requested. The police had questioned her extensively after the attempt on his life. It was a sorry state of affairs when a man was forced to face the fact that his own wife might be guilty of wanting his demise. Once he would have dismissed that notion as absurd, but truth to tell, he no longer knew what she would do.

"I'll ring for her," he said. Using the intercom connected to the phone, he called his wife.

She answered sleepily, irritation in her voice. Joe

told her Thaddeus was with him in the den and she was needed. A long pause ensued, then she informed him she would be a few minutes.

Forcing a smile, he told the other two men Meredith would be there in about twenty minutes.

He was fifteen minutes short on his estimation.

She swept into the den on a wave of the expensive perfume he'd given her last Christmas. Her black pantsuit was elegant, as were all her clothes. Gone were the days of jeans and sneakers, of running in the sun, her laughter teasing him and the children as they chased after her.

"Coffee?" he asked, suppressing the memories that haunted him more and more of late as the new generation married and had children of their own. The lonely path of old age loomed before him.

"Please." She studied Thaddeus disdainfully. "What are you doing here? Have you found Emily?"

"No, ma'am," the detective replied in his polite manner. "It's about a different matter."

Neither the gravity of the lawman's voice nor his impressive size appeared to intimidate Meredith. She accepted the cup and sat gracefully on the loveseat, her eyebrows raised slightly as she waited for the lawman to continue, her manner regal. Joe found it embarrassing. The old Meredith, the woman he remembered, or maybe had fantasized, would have been warmly welcoming.

"Mrs. Colton, do you have any idea where your twin now resides?"

The coffee splashed all over the table and rug as the cup fell with a clatter into its saucer. She stared at the detective, at first seemingly horrified, then her face became livid with anger. "Why are you prying into my past?" she demanded instead of answering the odd question.

"We investigate everyone who might have a motive in murder," he explained calmly. "Our records show there were two daughters born to your parents—twin girls, Meredith and Patsy. Checking further, we also discovered that Patsy Portman was once incarcerated for murder. At eighteen, she killed the man who was father to her child."

"My God," Joe muttered, shocked almost to stupefaction by the news. He automatically sopped up the spilled coffee with several napkins, his mind reeling at the revelations.

Glancing at Drake, Joe felt a deep sorrow. While he had been disillusioned about his wife long ago, it was still a sad day when a child lost faith in a parent. But there was no time to dwell on it and no way to protect his son, Joe realized. Drake was a man, one who'd seen his share of trouble in the world.

"Later," Thaddeus went on relentlessly, "she was transferred to a clinic for the..." Here, he did pause for an instant. "...insane."

Joe exhaled sharply as shock rolled over him again.

"Mother, is this true?" Drake broke in, disbelief rampant as he tried to comprehend this new development.

Aware of his own disjointed thoughts, he glanced at his father, afraid such news would give the older man a heart attack. His father looked resigned, almost defeated, his expression the bleakest Drake had ever witnessed.

His mother glared at him. "What of it? It had nothing to do with me. Nothing!"

Drake shook his head as the realization sank in that the police report was accurate, that this wasn't some kind of bad joke.

"Where is she, this twin you've never bothered to mention?" Joe asked, his voice low and hoarse, the strain evident in the way he held himself.

Suddenly her composure crumpled and she put her hands over her face. "She's dead. She's been dead for years."

Drake and Joe looked to Thaddeus for confirmation. The detective shrugged. "Mrs. Colton, is there anything to verify your sister's death, such as hospital records or a burial site?"

Drake recoiled from his mother's expression when she lifted her head. She looked almost insane, as feral as a house cat gone wild, her eyes glinting dangerously. Then she smiled triumphantly and the impression was gone.

"Wait, I remember something!" She leaped to her feet. "I have a letter from the clinic, the St. James Clinic. I can get it. I've kept it all these years."

When she dashed into the hall, the lawman followed. Drake glanced at his father. Both of them went after the other two. The day's revelations apparently weren't over.

Both he and his father pressed close as Thaddeus read the letter, which was on the clinic's letterhead. It offered condolences over Patsy Portman's death and spoke of her unhappy state of mind and suggested she had gone on to a more peaceful life than the one the young woman had led here on Earth. The body had been cremated and the ashes scattered in the Pacific, as she had requested.

"She blamed me," Meredith said when the three men looked at her. "I wouldn't lie for her at the trial. She said I had betrayed her."

"Why didn't you ever tell us, tell *me* about her?" Joe asked, his face as grim as a death mask.

"Patsy begged me not to tell anyone about her. Later, after she'd been at the clinic for several months, she said she wanted the family to forget she ever existed, that her life was nothing—"

With a little cry of despair, she swayed and reached out a hand toward them. Drake caught her before she fell into a faint.

"Put her on the bed," Joe said. "I'll tend to her."

"I need to keep the letter, sir," Thaddeus said after they had made Meredith as comfortable as they could. "To go in the file."

Nodding, Joe covered his wife with an afghan. Drake brought a damp cloth from the bathroom and laid it on her forehead. "I'll get Inez."

"Yes, please," his father said. "Then I want to talk to Thaddeus and clarify a few more details."

After learning all that was known from the detective, Drake went to his own room to sort through his mixed-up thoughts and impressions. One thing for sure—his homecomings were becoming more and more fraught with surprises.

After thinking things over, then making sure his

mother was still in bed, the housekeeper with her, he checked the time. It was past noon back East. He picked up the phone and dialed Washington, D.C.

His brother's wife and research assistant answered the law office number on the first ring.

"Lucy? This is Drake. Is Rand available?"

"Well, hello! Yes, I'll put him right on."

Drake liked his older brother's new wife. She didn't waste a lot of time on chitchat and foolish questions.

"Hey, bro," Rand said a minute later. "Where are you?"

"At the family homestead," Drake said with more than a trace of irony. "We've had some interesting disclosures here this morning."

"Oh?" Rand said, detectable caution in the word.

"There's more to our mother than meets the eye." Drake informed Rand of the lawman's visit, the shocking news, the letter concerning the death and their mother's fainting spell. "Comments?" he finished.

Rand cleared his throat. "I was the one who sent Dad the message that Emily was okay."

This non sequitur gave Drake pause. Knowing his brother and that there had to be a connection, he asked, "You've been in contact with her?"

"Yeah. She asked me not to reveal her whereabouts. I'd tell you, but, uh, not over the phone."

"Good thinking," Drake agreed. "The way things stand, I don't trust anything or anyone right now."

"Listen, Drake, you remember that Em thought there were two Merediths—the good one and the evil one—back when she and Mom were in that car wreck?''

A chill swept up Drake's neck. "Yeah."

"This confirms that possibility, doesn't it?"

Drake muttered an expletive. "I can't believe..." He let the thought trail off. The problem was, he could believe in the weird possibility that their mother was an impostor.

Rand picked up on the idea. "The evil twin. Seems like something out of a bad movie."

"You believe Emily?"

His brother let out a loud sigh. "Enough that I've had Austin McGrath check into Mother's background."

"You knew and didn't say a word?" Drake demanded, realizing why his brother hadn't sounded surprised. "You knew about the twin...and the murder?"

"And the clinic for the insane, yes," Rand confirmed. "Lucy found out recently. I've had a bit more time to absorb this, but believe me, I was as shocked as you and Dad. I've asked Austin to see if he could find out what happened to the twin, but so far, no trace. I suppose, if she's dead, there isn't more to find out."

"*If* she's dead?"

Rand didn't immediately reply. "What if Mother's dead and her twin took her place? That would explain Em's vision of two Merediths."

Drake released a pent-up breath. "The implications are pretty awful."

"Yeah. Mother may have been murdered."

"Ten years with all of us living with an impostor? Surely Dad would have guessed... No, it's too bizarre."

"I, uh, don't believe our parents have slept together in a number of years. They've had separate bedrooms since, well, I can't remember when, but a long time."

"Yeah, that's right, since before Teddy was born. I remember being kind of shocked when I came home one time and found out." Drake cursed again.

"Same here," Rand said in understanding. "Lucy and I have gone over this in every detail. We think Em is onto something. The question is, what?"

Drake thought for a minute. "With identical twins, you can't tell who's who from a DNA test, right?"

"Right. Not unless there was something that was traceable in the blood, such as an immunity to some rare disease that the other hadn't been exposed to."

After an hour of speculation and surmises, they decided they needed more information. "Keep me posted on anything Austin finds out," Drake said. "I'll let you know what happens on this end."

"Will do."

"You know what bothers me? If this woman, this evil twin, took Mother's place, does that mean she ran Mom and Emily off the road, killed Mom and hid the body somewhere near the wreck, then pretended to be the good sister?"

Rand paused only a second. "That's what Emily believes. She thinks the evil twin hired someone to kill *her* because of her memories of the accident. She also thinks the same person was hired to kill Dad."

Drake briefly closed his eyes and pinched the

bridge of his nose. "It just keeps getting worse and worse, doesn't it?"

"Yes. Drake? Be careful," Rand advised, causing the hair on Drake's neck to prickle. "How long are you in for?"

"I have a two-month leave. I can take more for a family emergency if needed. Did you know Maya is, uh, pregnant?"

"Dad mentioned it," Rand admitted, a touch of humor in his voice for the first time. "Forgive me for being indelicate, but could it be yours?"

"Yeah, but I haven't wrung a confession out of her. You know how stubborn women can be."

"Mmm, are you two getting married?"

"Well, I've offered. She thinks marriage would be a mistake." Drake thought of the warm, loving Maya of eight months ago. It caused his insides to ache in ways he couldn't explain. Not that he would tell his brother or anyone else the strange pangs he felt around Maya.

"I can identify with that," Rand admitted with a low chuckle. "Tell her I said to stop being so damn stubborn. I want my niece or nephew properly in the family."

"It's a girl," Drake said, his tone a lot lighter than he felt. "I'll give her your sage advice. Give your Lucy and Max my regards."

Rand promised he would and hung up. Drake pulled on a coat and went outside. Action was required. A walk on the beach would blow away the cobwebs in his head.

The sky was overcast, the air heavy with the chill

moisture brought down from Alaska on the ocean currents as he crossed the patio. He headed down the sloping lawn toward the cliffs where the low cloud bank obscured the shore in a haze of mist. He nearly fell over a figure sitting on the steps leading to the shore.

"What the hell?" he exclaimed.

"I'm sorry. I didn't hear you," Maya said, huddling deeper into a dark wool shawl that all but obliterated her.

The cold place inside him warmed slightly. He dropped down to the step beside her. "Are you all right?"

"Yes. I just came out for a breath of air and to be alone—" She stopped as if this confession might be construed as a weakness on her part.

"I was feeling the same. I needed some thinking time."

She started to rise. "I'll leave you to it."

He caught her arm. "Don't go. I have something I want to ask."

Her beautiful dark eyes turned toward him, suspicion in their depths. Once she had looked at him in total trust. Eight months ago. It seemed a lifetime.

"You've known my family all your life—"

"Yes?" she said when he stopped.

"Have you noticed anything different about my mother during that time? Do you think she's changed?"

She stared first at him, then out at the swirling mist covering the sea. "Everyone changes with time."

He made an impatient sound. "Yes, but not dras-

tically. Values stay generally the same. And disposi-
tion. Have her moods, her way of behaving, changed
a lot?''

"Have they to you?''

He considered the past. "Yes. When I was a kid,
we used to ride and play games and picnic on the
beach. Later…things were different here. But I was
away at college and was never really home except for
brief periods after that.''

Maya nodded. "I do remember her as warmer,
friendlier. Lana and I weren't allowed to intrude on
your family and with the age differences between us
kids, we didn't play much together.''

"Except for the baseball games when we rounded
up everyone we could find to make up two teams,''
he reminded her. "You were a good player. For a
girl.''

He felt somewhat better when she flashed him a
brief smile, then gazed back at the sea. "As an em-
ployee, I see Ms. Meredith differently than you would
as a child of the family. Rank and privilege and all
that,'' she said lightly.

"Right. Cinderella and Prince Charming.'' He
couldn't help the sarcasm. She got to him faster than
any female he'd ever met.

A blush tinged her smooth cheeks.

"Is that what you think of our family, that we're a
bunch of snobs?''

"Of course not. Your father is a wonderful person.
He's never made anyone feel less than a friend.''

"But the same can't be said of my mother?''

She was silent.

"And me? How do you see me?" he demanded, his voice going husky as he was consumed by a need to know.

He touched her hair, which was damp with the mist, its waves deep and enticing. Hunger sprang to life, driving out all but the need to bury himself in her and forget the current perplexities in his world. Except she was part of them. He withdrew his hand reluctantly.

Twisting, she faced him, her eyes level with his. "You're a man used to going his own way. Alone."

"A person can get tired of being alone," he said, surprising himself as much as her. Reaching out, he ran his fingertips along her cheek, then under her chin and tilted her face up a bit. Her lips were naturally pink and luscious. Kissable.

"Maya," he murmured.

Some of the need and confusion he felt after the revealing morning must have shown in his eyes.

"Please don't," she whispered.

But he couldn't help himself. He slipped his hand into her hair and behind her head and pulled her forward as he leaned toward her. Heat flooded through him, melting the cold, achy place. With the heat came the need, the fierce but scary need that he couldn't afford to feel. A man with no future couldn't afford tender feelings.

"Don't need you? Don't want you?" he questioned. "It would be easier to cut off my right arm. I keep remembering last summer and the way it was. I want it like that again."

She shook her head, her face closed against him.

With fingers that trembled, he turned her toward him. Her eyes were misty with tears. She closed them and held very still, as if she were trapped there, somewhere between the devil and the deep blue sea.

And he was the devil.

"Ah, God," he said and realized it really was a prayer. He just didn't know for what. "I never meant to hurt you."

"You didn't. It—it was only my own foolish dreams that did that."

She tried to turn away again, but he wouldn't, couldn't, let her. There were things to be said between them. There was the child's future to think of.

"I've made a will," he said. "You and the child are my heirs. I've saved some money since I got out of college and there's a trust fund from my parents for each of us kids."

That got her attention. She turned on him angrily. "I don't want your money! How dare— That you would even think— As if money could—" She collected herself with a visible effort. "I don't need your money. I can take care of myself and the baby."

She looked so fierce, so insulted, so damn beautiful, he couldn't stop what happened next. He kissed her.

As if he were dying and she was the breath of life. As if he couldn't get enough of her. As if he would never let her go.

When she struggled to rise, he rose with her, continuing the wild, foolish kiss that his heart demanded.

Curving his body around her rounded tummy, he felt their child kick vigorously, whether in delight or protest, he didn't know. A surge of pride rolled into the passion he couldn't suppress. She stood stiffly in his arms. He eased the kiss but couldn't quite give it up yet.

Suddenly, she softened and with a little moan, laid her hands on his chest, to touch him, he realized. She wasn't pushing him away. Triumph blazed in him.

Folding her in his arms, he savored the smoothness of her lips, the sweetness of her mouth. Eight months of dreams narrowed to this single moment of bliss.

He ran his hands up and down her back and into the thick waves of her hair. The tactile sense of her, the taste and scent, the bliss of her being, her existence, fed that inner place where need dwelt. He slanted his mouth this way and that upon her lips.

Maya fought against responding, but it was useless. This was Drake. He was part of her life, of her dreams and expectations of the future. She sensed the powerful hunger in his lean, hard frame. More than that, she knew there were feelings between them. They had shared too much to be indifferent. But was need enough?

She sighed when he moved down her throat, pulling her shawl aside to place random kisses on her neck. Putting her arms around him, she rubbed his shoulders and into his hair, soothing something raw and hurting in him almost the way she would have had he been one of the youngest Colton boys.

However, her body reacted far differently. Drake was a man, and she responded as a woman to him. She wanted the passion and the fire. She'd missed his arms and the strength of his body surrounding hers in heady desire. She'd missed the hot, hot hunger that blazed to life at the slightest touch between them.

Resting against the railing, she let the kiss take her to that place of dreams and hopes. If only love could be enough, she thought sadly, and realized it wasn't. Only Drake could overcome the strange darkness she sensed within him. Only he could take that one giant step forward into the sunshine of life. He had to want a future in order for there to be one.

Tears crowded behind her closed eyes. She wanted so much for him...for them and their little girl.

"Marry me," he whispered, raising his head and staring into her eyes as if he would control her with his will.

She shook her head. "I can't."

"Why? Dammit, why?"

"You have to want it, too."

"I do."

"You don't. Not really."

He gripped her shoulders, but his touch remained gentle. "If not for us, then for *her*," he said, grabbing whatever argument he could, fair or not. He ran his hands over her abdomen.

She looked at him in mute despair, shredding his heart into confusion and anger and lots of other things.

"You want me," he reminded her, slipping his hands inside the shawl and touching her breasts, taking their weight and measuring their fullness in his palms.

Maya couldn't lie. "Yes, but sometimes a person wants too much."

"Such as?" he asked almost absently, as if his entire attention was focused on her body and its changes as he explored her new contours.

"I don't know," she admitted with a tiny gasp as her nipples contracted swiftly, painfully.

The familiar heat flamed in her. The delicious softening of her body and her will followed.

Drake felt no flash of triumph as she yielded to the passion between them. The feelings were too deep for that, going beyond anything he'd ever experienced with any woman. That was what had put him on the run last June, sending him scurrying off on the dangerous mission in relief. Thinking, planning, acting— those things had kept the turbulent emotions at bay. For a while.

"You make me vulnerable," he accused. "I can't afford that. It's not good for my job."

"Or your life. Need puts a person at risk."

He experienced the jab of truth in her words. On some level, she seemed to know him better than he knew himself. "Yes. A man has to think carefully and plan ahead."

Maya caressed his cheeks. "But the feelings are there, Drake, whether you acknowledge them or not. You have to learn to live with them."

He frowned. Confusion darted through his eyes. She smiled with a sadness that went soul deep. Although she wasn't exactly sure what she meant, she knew Drake had to come to terms with his inner self before he could take on a wife and child. She didn't even know how she had come by this knowledge, but it was there, inside her, all the same.

Slowly he let her go, his expression grim and now closed to her. "Go," he said hoarsely. "Go before I take you to the alcove whether you want to come or not."

"I know you better than that, and you don't know yourself at all if you think you might force me."

"I could make you want to go willingly," he said in blunt honesty.

She shook her head. "If I come to you, it will be by my will, none other. You wouldn't accept less."

"I'd accept whatever you would give."

"Go find your soul, Drake. Then come to me and share your heart." She managed a smile.

Touching his mouth gently, she told him silently of her love, which had never died, she now knew, then she turned and walked up the steps and across the lawn to her lonely room. If she were going to make a future for the baby, she had to study.

Five

"Uh, you going to town this morning?" Drake asked the housekeeper as she bustled out of the house, struggling to pull on a jacket. She'd gone to town for groceries every Thursday morning for as long as he could remember.

She stopped and smiled at him, the usual affection in her eyes. Drake felt immediately better.

"Yes," she said. "I have to get groceries for this crew. They insist on eating several times a day."

Drake managed a chuckle and held the jacket for her. "Okay if I ride along?"

Her dark eyes raked over his face, but she nodded without asking about the vintage pickup he'd bought and restored to gleaming perfection years ago. He walked to the ranch wagon and climbed in when she did.

"Maya will be along in a moment," Inez informed him. "She had errands, too, and volunteered to help with the groceries."

His heart leaped about, banging off the walls of his chest until he got it under control again. Glancing to the side, he saw Maya emerge from the main house, then hesitate when her eyes met his. He sensed her reluctance even as she walked forward. He jumped out of the station wagon and held the door.

"Your chariot awaits," he said, not very originally but suddenly his mind couldn't get a grasp on words.

She nodded curtly and slid inside. He did the same.

"What are you doing?" she demanded, forced to scoot over so he could get in.

"Drake needs a ride to town," Inez explained. She put the car in gear and started off.

"Here's your seat belt," Drake said and helped Maya into the contraption, careful to place it below the swell of her abdomen. He repressed an urge to caress her there and fastened his own seat belt instead.

Inez chatted on the way to Prosperino, but Maya sat in stubborn silence, a disapproving frown on her face. Drake responded to the housekeeper's remarks, his entire left side burning from Maya's nearness.

Last night, after she'd gone to her room and closed the door, he'd roamed the house, unable to settle for thinking about her remarks out on the cliff stairs.

Find his soul? How? Where did a person begin looking?

He thought of the darkness deep within. Was that where his soul resided? If so, it was a place he didn't want to disturb. It brought nothing but memories and pain.

Haunted by her advice and rejection, he'd fled his room at midnight and drove to town.

After a couple of beers—okay, maybe three or four—at the local bar, he'd run into Thaddeus Law at the door. The lawman had insisted on taking him home, thinking he'd had one too many.

It occurred to Drake that Maya knew of the incident and that was why every glance was filled with disapproval.

"I was in town last night for an hour or so," he said, watching for a reaction. "I needed to get away and…think about things."

"I heard," Inez told him when her daughter failed to acknowledge his statement. "Heather said Thaddeus brought you home. That's how I knew you'd be wanting to pick up the truck this morning."

Maya had already heard Heather, Thaddeus Law's bride and Joe Colton's personal assistant, teasing Drake about his big night out on the town while she set the table for breakfast that morning. What he did was his business, she'd reminded herself, ignoring the jab of worry.

"I stumbled coming out the door, so ol' Thaddeus decided I'd had one too many," Drake said on a note of exasperation and amusement. "He was determined, and it was easier to go along with him than fight."

"Thaddeus is a naturally protective man," Inez said. "Since he married Heather he's been even more concerned with solving the mysteries involving the Colton family." She paused. "Especially Emily's whereabouts. I have to admit to worrying about her, a child off on her own like that.''

Maya felt the quick tightening of Drake's muscles, then the deliberate way he relaxed as he agreed with her mother about the detective's attitude and the concern over Emily. She stole a glance at him.

His gaze met hers, but absently, as if he were lost in thought. He didn't seem too worried about his sister, which wasn't like him. Drake was also a protective person, and Emily was only twenty. She'd left the ranch with only the clothes on her back and not much else.

''You know something,'' she said on a sudden hunch.

''I know Emily is okay. I talked to Rand yesterday.''

Maya gasped. ''Has she been in contact with Rand?''

Drake didn't answer right away. Maya felt the hurt of his distrust in sharing information with her and her mother for an instant before he decided to tell them the truth.

''She called him,'' Drake admitted. ''Rand asked Austin McGrath to check into things.''

''Then…then you believe Emily's story about the two Merediths?'' Inez asked, her manner also hesitant.

''Do you?'' he challenged.

Maya glanced from one to the other, aware that both knew more than she did about the strange events on the ranch during the past few months. She'd been caught up in her own troubles, not to mention the shock of being pregnant.

Her mother thought carefully before answering. "A person can change over time, I suppose, but…" She didn't continue, but looked troubled by her musings.

"But Mother changed too much," he concluded.

"Perhaps, but who knows another's heart?"

Maya considered the implications of his questions and Emily's belief she'd seen two Merediths for a brief spell after the car accident years ago. Finally she said, "This person…she would have to be a twin to successfully take another's place for so long, wouldn't she? I mean, how could she fool everyone, including her own husband and children, without a close connection?"

"There was a twin. That's the news Thaddeus brought us yesterday. Mother admits to having one, but she has a letter that also claims the twin died long ago."

The shock of this information reverberated through Maya. Ms. Meredith had actually had a twin? It was mind-boggling, to say the least. "No one knew about her?"

"No."

"That must make things even more confusing," Inez said, her manner one of sympathy.

Maya wasn't sure what she felt. She couldn't imagine a husband not recognizing his wife or children somehow not knowing their mother wasn't the true one.

"It's damn strange," Drake conceded. His gaze

flicked to her again. "Another mystery to be solved, it seems."

Maya bit back a retort about there being no mystery between them. That he could think for a minute the baby might not be his after their time together was an insult beyond forgiving. It spoke to her of his reluctance to accept any part of her and the child. He didn't want it to be his.

She breathed carefully, deeply, until the hurt of that fact receded. Laying a hand on her tummy, she assured the baby that *she* wanted her. Drake laid his hand over hers, startling her.

His gaze held a haunted quality, as if he asked her forgiveness. She looked away.

They arrived in town and went in different directions. Maya did her shopping, then met her mother at the grocery to help her carry the ranch staples out. Drake was there, already helping, his manner easy as he chatted with the housekeeper.

She had to admit he had never acted as if her parents were less than wonderful and an equal to the Coltons in every way. There was some comfort in that. And in the fact that he hadn't been inebriated the previous night. She would never put up with a man with vile habits.

Not that she would have to put up with anything from him. It would never come to marriage between them. He would have to go back to his dangerous career soon, then he could forget her and the baby, knowing he'd come home and offered to do the honorable thing.

Ignoring the dark mood, she sighed and pressed her

hands to her back. If she got through this month and the one after, then she would get her life on track and…all would be well.

She fought the harsh sting of tears that threatened to overcome her. One thing she would be glad to get rid of was this ridiculous urge to cry at the least little thing.

"Ride with me," Drake requested, materializing beside her while she stood lost in her thoughts.

"I have to get back. I've got a test coming up."

"We'll go straight to the ranch," he promised.

Before she could think of a good excuse, her mother got in the ranch wagon and drove off, leaving them standing in the parking lot. "It seems I have no choice," she said.

"Don't be angry with your mother. I told her I would bring you. I want to talk—"

"I have nothing to say." She gathered her ragged composure around her, forming a wall to ward off any softer feelings that would overcome her better judgment.

"Then you can listen."

Looking grim as death, he took her arm and led her to the truck. There, he helped her inside by lifting her with hands at her waist, his touch as gentle as possible. Again the need to weep overcame her. She stared straight ahead while he drove out of town.

"I talked to your father," he said after a mile of silence. "I gave him a copy of my will so it will be handy if anything happens to me."

The idea caused such a pang in her heart she had

to wrap her arms across her chest to contain the hurt. "Nothing will," she said hoarsely. "You're careful."

He laughed without humor. "I wasn't very careful with you," he reminded her.

She had no retort for that.

"Maya, I know the baby is mine," he said quite gently.

"How? I was dating someone else when you came home last summer. There may have been a whole parade of men through my life, for all you know."

"Maybe, but you were a virgin the first time we made love."

"You can't know that for sure."

"I know inexperience when I see it. You hadn't the foggiest notion of how to proceed."

Her face flamed at the knowing look in the glance he gave her before turning his eyes back to the road. She had put that knowledge there and nothing she could do would dispel it.

He turned in at the ranch drive and slowed almost to a crawl before going off the road and parking among the bay trees and willow shrubs beside the seasonal creek.

"You were trembling," he continued, turning to her and laying an arm on the back of the seat. "So was I."

She flashed him a quelling look which did nothing to shut him up. She hated remembering how gullible she'd been.

"I'd never made love before—"

"Oh, right," she scoffed, ignoring the note of wonder and longing in his tone that jarred right to the center of her being. She wouldn't be so foolish as to fall under his spell again.

"I'd had sex," he said in a harsher tone, "but not...not what we shared."

Maya clenched her hands together. "Don't. You don't have to say that."

"I think I do," he murmured. "I hurt you when I asked about the baby. I knew it was mine. I just needed to hear you say it. Men sometimes need assurance, you know."

She shook her head.

He ignored it. "I'm not surprised we produced a child. What we shared was too strong not to have lasting results. I'm not sorry, either, except for the shame—"

She rounded on him in fury. "Getting pregnant by the son of the house may be one of the oldest clichés in the book, but I'm not ashamed! I may be the housekeeper's daughter, but what I did, I did for—"

"For love," he finished when she stopped abruptly, appalled at nearly giving herself away so completely.

"It was madness," she said stubbornly. "Moonlight and madness. That was all."

His gaze told her he knew better. "I seem to be saying this all wrong, but I wanted you to know I plan to take care of my own. This baby is mine. I intend to see that she never needs for anything."

The fierce pain that had taken up residence inside her since reading his note of farewell eased somewhat. She nodded stiffly.

"And don't ever bring up the fact that your mother is the housekeeper again," he added with a warning frown. "It has never played a part in our relationship. As far as I'm concerned, it never will."

"I know. I'm sorry I said that. It was hateful."

He grinned, surprising her. His fingers touched her shoulders and rested there. "Well, we're making progress, it seems. Perhaps we should stop while we're ahead." Still smiling he started the truck and turned around.

At the house, Maya left Drake and hurried to her room where she flipped on the computer. She felt the weight of her studies and responsibilities as she edited a paper and sent it via the Internet to her teacher at the university in San Francisco. Taking her textbook with her, she went out to the vacant sunroom and read the assigned chapter, then made notes and laid the book down.

Moving the chair to the recliner position, she closed her eyes and fell into a light slumber.

That was where Drake found Maya when he came inside shortly before three. He took a seat in a comfortable padded chair and sipped the fresh coffee Inez had made, his gaze ever drawn to the woman who slept with a slight frown on her face, as if her dreams troubled her.

He knew about dreams. Of late, his were all mixed up with babies and cars that came careening around curves, running over women and children without pause. It didn't take a genius to figure out what had prompted them.

Coward. He grimly acknowledged this fact. It took less courage to face an enemy's gun than it took to face this woman and her demand that he find his soul, then share his heart. The dark place hammered inside him like a demon demanding its due as he admitted this fact.

Stretching out on the sofa, he wondered what marriage would be like. Coming home to Maya every night. Holding her. Making love. Sharing the tenderness and TLC she bestowed on his younger brothers...

Maya woke with a start and glanced wildly around the room. Drake opened his eyes and sat up. She realized he'd been asleep on the sofa while she slept in the recliner.

"Maya!" Teddy yelled again.

"In here," she called in a softer voice, rising.

The two boys rushed into the sunroom. "Hi, Drake. Say, can we try roping again?" Joe Junior asked.

"Not today," Maya cut in before Drake could answer. "I think you have something for me."

Teddy handed over his report card willingly, but the older boy had a hard time finding his in his book bag. When Maya saw it, she understood why.

"Oh, Joe," she said.

He hung his head. "I sort of didn't do so good on the math exam. I, uh, got mixed up on percents."

Maya's stomach went through the falling-elevator syndrome. Ms. Meredith was going to be furious when she saw the C minus on Joe's report card for the six-week period. Nothing but As were acceptable, a B at the very least.

"We'll go over the test questions," she said to her young charge. "Did you bring the paper home?"

"Yes. Uh, I guess we'd better go change clothes and do some studying now."

"I think that would be an excellent idea."

"Can I stay with Drake?" Teddy asked.

"You'd better go with your brother," Drake said. "I have other things to do now. We'll work on your roping this weekend. If that's okay with Maya."

Before she could answer, Maya heard footsteps in the hall. Her heart did its falling act again. "Are the boys home?" Ms. Meredith said, coming into the room.

Her eyes lit up on seeing her youngest sons. She held out her arms. "Come give me a kiss, or are you too big to be kind to your mother?"

Maya stayed silent while the boys dutifully kissed their mother on each cheek, then reported on their day.

"Isn't this report card day?" Meredith asked.

Joe and Teddy edged toward the hallway, hoping for the sanctuary of their rooms before the revealing of grades.

"You boys go change while I speak to your nanny," their mother said, taking a seat and holding out her hand.

With relieved looks, they raced off while Maya handed over the teachers' reports. She steeled herself while her employer studied the grades.

"What is that?" Meredith demanded. "What is this grade in math?"

"Joe says he got mixed up on the percentage problems. We'll go over them this weekend—"

Meredith slapped the reports on the coffee table.

"I pay you to see that they do their lessons and understand them properly."

"I'm sorry," Maya answered carefully, keeping her tone neutral. "We'll go over the problems—"

"I told Joe hiring someone without any training or skills was a mistake, but he insisted on it because you needed the money, as if we don't pay your parents enough—"

"Mother," Drake broke into the tirade, "I'm sure each person on the ranch earns his or her own salary. Maya has helped with the boys since she was hardly more than a girl herself. Overall, I'd say she's done an excellent job."

Meredith rounded on her second son, her demeanor icily forbidding. "Are you an expert in child care? I didn't know the SEALs taught that as well as other abilities."

Her gaze went disdainfully to Maya's rounded figure. Embarrassment spread through Maya at the obvious reference. She glanced at Drake, who studied his mother with frigid intensity, the small scar on his chin white with fury.

Startled, she realized how much alike the two were. Both had light brown hair with golden highlights, Meredith's enhanced by an artful hair stylist. Their eyes were an identical brown, both with flecks that gleamed like molten gold when the light hit them just right.

And now, in their anger, they both displayed the same fury, the same icy control. Chills ran along Maya's scalp.

"Once I learned kindness," he said softly, "from a woman I admired a great deal. Once."

Hatred seemed to blaze from his mother's eyes, then it was gone before Maya was certain she saw it.

"The world would be a better place if there was more kindness, wouldn't it?" she said, her voice filled with mockery, then she left the room, the click of her heels sounding smartly on the marble tiles in the foyer as she left the house.

"I'd better see about the boys," Maya said and rushed for the hall to the north wing of the sprawling house.

Drake took two steps and caught her arm. "I'm sorry," he said, his manner gentle.

"For what?" His touch soothed the insult of his mother's words. She wanted to lean against him and let him comfort her. Only she was pretty sure where that would lead. More and more, she wanted to accept the passion that bloomed between them. It *was* madness.

His smile was sad, sort of ironic. "I'm not sure. For Mother, I suppose, and her attitude."

"It doesn't matter. I'm used to it. I mean...I don't think she means to be unkind. She's just concerned about the boys."

He dropped his hand, leaving a cold place on her arm. "I won't stand by and see our child hurt by careless words, no matter who they come from."

"You shouldn't quarrel with your family because of me," she said, filled with concern. "Family is important."

"Marissa is my family now."

The solid declaration threw her off balance. Staring into his eyes, she saw the darkness, but there was also a tender element—his care for their unborn child.

Quickly, before she lost her head completely, she rushed from the room and down the hall to check on her two young charges...and to give her heart a chance to settle down before she did something incredibly stupid, like fling herself into Drake's arms and beg to stay there. At that moment, she would have agreed to marriage and anything else he suggested.

However, one of them had to be practical, she reminded herself later that night after the boys were asleep and she did her usual pacing until her back eased enough for sleep. But it was hard, so hard, when all she wanted was his arms, holding her safe in a world she no longer trusted.

In Mississippi, the woman who now called herself Louise Smith but apparently had been known as Patsy Portman in the past, woke with a start. Overhead, the thunder rolled again. She flung herself out of bed and pulled on a warm robe as the chill of the February night and the storm roiled around her. Going to the door, she opened it and stared into the dark.

She realized it had all been a dream, the recurring nightmare in which she heard a child cry out for help.

Shaken at the realness of the dream, she locked the door and sank into a nearby chair.

Who are you?

She'd asked the question before and as usual, she never found an answer in the swirling fog of her mind. She only knew there was a child somewhere, one she'd let down in some way she couldn't remember, just as there was a dark man in her past and a fountain and an indescribable joy.

Burying her face in her hands, she wept, her heart in pieces. "I can't take it anymore," she whispered. "I can't. I can't. I can't."

She repeated the words the next day to Martha Wilkes, who had become her friend as well as her psychologist while trying to help her regain her memory. Martha was a lovely black woman who had worked her way out of poverty and whose quiet perseverance was an inspiration to Louise.

"Then let it go," Martha advised.

Louise frowned at the other woman. "Just like that?"

"Yes. Sometimes the mind needs a rest. I think you've reached that point. I've found patients sometimes remember everything after they've given themselves permission to ease up. It might work for you."

"It bothers me that someone might be in trouble, that they might need me," Louise said. "Last night, the dream was different. The girl was older, a woman now, but still afraid of something. Or somebody."

Martha nodded. "Your mind could be adjusting for the years that have passed since the last time you saw her."

"I think the girl is mine. Sometimes I can see her so clearly. She has red hair, blue eyes and dimples. I think she called me 'mommy' in one of the dreams."

"And the dark man?"

Louise shook her head sadly. "I don't know, but there's this great peace and joy when he appears. And there's this wonderful place with a fountain and sunshine and the most beautiful garden. My own version of paradise, I suppose,'' she finished with a laugh that echoed the sadness in her heart.

"Give it a rest,'' Martha reiterated.

"I think I'm going to have to. I just can't keep searching and getting nowhere. And yet, sometimes I feel so close to the edge. Like last night during the storm. I actually went to the door, positive I would see this girl—woman—standing there, calling for me. Why can't I remember? Why?''

"We can try hypnosis and regression once more,'' Martha suggested, but doubtfully.

"I can't get past the day I woke up at the clinic in California. I don't know what I was doing out there when it appears I lived in a trailer park here at one time.''

Martha shook her head. "I read over your record last week. Maybe it would shed some light if we had all your old records, but they were destroyed by fire. I have reached one conclusion.''

Louise looked a question at her friend.

"Whatever you may have been in the past, you are not bipolar at the present, nor do you suffer from multiple personality disorder as the records suggest. Other than the memory loss, I'd say you're one of the most balanced people I've ever known. Sometimes I wonder if there were two of you, one who was mentally unstable and another who was not.''

Louise smiled ironically. "Which one am I, Doctor?''

"Oh, you're sane enough," Martha assured her. "Could you have had a twin?"

"Well, if I did, I haven't seen *her* in my nightmares."

"I wish we had the old records. Those could tell us so much. If we only knew for sure that you were born fifty-two years ago in California, then we might find out about your family."

"It sounds crazy that I can't remember the year or the place I was born."

"Patience," the doctor advised, her frown changing to a smile. "Time is on our side."

"But what about that of the red-haired girl? Last night I had a terrible feeling time was running out for her."

"Let's work on your problem first. I want you to mentally say 'No!' each time you start worrying about your past. Refuse to let your conscious mind dwell on it. We'll let your subconscious work on the task in the background. Meanwhile, you're to relax and have some fun. What happened to that guy you were dating?"

"He's a friend, but that's all. Without a past, I'm not sure I have a future."

"I don't want to hear that kind of talk. At some point, you'll have to get on with your life, with memories or without. That's the way life is."

Out on the storm-swept street, Louise admitted the doctor was right, but something inside her, in her heart, said there was once a great love in her life.

"Come back to me," she whispered to the dark

lover from her past. "No!" she said, recalling her instructions.

But warmth spread through her as she zipped her jacket against the wind.

Six

"**Y**ou don't have time for roping," Maya reminded the boys Saturday morning. "Mr. Martin will be here soon."

Joe Junior and Teddy gave her sullen glances, reverting to the spoiled brats they became when their mother overindulged them as she did in moments of frenzied attention. Last night had been an example. Ms. Meredith had let them have extra dessert before bedtime, then had countermanded Maya's orders for bed and let them stay up late to watch a movie not suited to their ages.

"I'll ask Mother," Joe said in a manner that made her want to shake him.

"She's visiting friends for the weekend," Joe Senior, said, coming into the living room from his den.

Drake was with him. "You would do well to mind Maya. Or would you rather be grounded for a week?"

The boys dropped their whiny manner. "No, sir," they both said respectfully.

Maya was relieved to hear a car approaching. "That must be Andy. We'll study in my room," she told the boys.

"Okay if the boys join me for some more roping after they finish their studies?" Drake asked.

Maya met his opaque gaze without flinching. "That will be fine. If they want to."

"Sure!" the boys shouted, sunny once more.

Maya hated the stiff, ill-at-ease way she sounded with Drake. But then, she'd never had a course in how to treat a former lover. Feeling huge, she turned and walked outside while her two charges headed down the hall to her room.

Joe Senior, watched the boys with a stern expression on his face while Drake fell into step with her, opening the front door and playing the gentleman, his handsome face solemn while shadows flickered through his eyes.

For a moment—one of total insanity—she wanted to take him into her arms and hold him…just hold him.

Eyes blurred, she nearly tripped on the step. Drake's arm was there immediately to catch her. His strength engulfed her and she felt safe, as if she'd sailed through stormy seas and found her haven at last. She closed her eyes as longing and need and a thousand other emotions churned through her.

"Maya," he murmured, sounding as desperate as she felt.

She blinked the too-ready tears away and gazed into his eyes. A mistake, that. She saw, for the briefest instant, his vulnerability and the unhappiness he hid behind his calm, capable manner.

Her heart banged against her ribcage, causing a pain similar to the one she'd felt when he'd told her of his twin's death.

"Maya," he said again.

She felt his need and her own and answered in the only way she knew how—by offering him the comfort of her touch. With trembling fingers, she gently caressed his shoulder.

A car door slammed. Every nerve in her body jumped, and she stepped back, back from the sheer craziness his touch induced in her heart. A shaky sigh escaped her.

Andy's face lit in a smile at seeing her, then sobered as he glanced at Drake. The muscles in his jaw hardened and he looked Drake over like a rival stag he'd like to dispatch with an angry charge, but he nodded politely. "Drake," he said by way of acknowledging the other man.

"Andy Martin, isn't it?" Drake said, equally polite.

"Yes. It's been a few years," Andy said.

"Since high-school football days. You were a couple of years behind me, as I recall."

"Three. Maya and I were classmates."

"If you're ready," Maya abruptly interrupted the exchange, keeping her eyes on Andy and ignoring

Drake. "Did you have time to research some problems for Johnny?"

"Yes. I'll get them. Uh, Mrs. Colton called and said her boys needed some help." His tone questioned Maya.

"Yes. Joe didn't do well on his exam in math. Can you tutor them on Saturdays, too?"

"Yes, it's already been arranged." His glance was apologetic.

Maya smiled to assure him she didn't mind that the boys' mother had gone over her head and dealt directly with Andy on the problem.

"Who's Johnny?" Drake wanted to know.

"I'm helping Maya tutor one of her Hopechest kids," Andy answered.

Maya explained about Johnny Collins and her concerns over him and her hopes for his future when Drake seemed interested in the boy.

"Let's bring him out to the ranch on Saturdays," he suggested. "He can study with the boys, then join us for roping lessons in the afternoon, if he'd like."

Maya considered. "That might be good. Skills in one area often translate into confidence in other areas. Johnny has good coordination and should do well."

"Great. Why don't we start today? How do I arrange to get him out to the ranch?"

"Let me get Joe and Teddy started with Andy, then I'll call the Hopechest. Ready?" she asked Andy.

He retrieved a briefcase from his car and followed her to her room where the two boys waited. They greeted their new tutor with less than enthusiasm.

Maya could relate to that. Feeling restless and agitated, she wanted freedom instead of responsibility.

Usually her seven-days-a-week duty didn't bother her, but she felt a need to get outside and walk until the nervous energy was dissipated and she could come to terms with the ridiculous emotions Drake generated in her rebellious heart. That organ needed a lecture on proper behavior around him.

Leaving Andy with the boys, she went to her mother's desk in the kitchen and called the children's ranch to see if Johnny could come out for the day.

Having arranged that, she realized she would have to tell Drake. She found him out in the corral. Like her, he expended his extra energy outdoors, this morning working with a golden gelding while River James observed.

Maya stopped at the railing beside River, the ranch foreman and a former foster child taken in by Joe and Meredith Colton years ago. River was now Drake's brother-in-law. Drake's sister, Sophie, had been pregnant when she and River had wed last summer. Maya stifled a sudden longing to seek out Sophie and confide her worries to the other woman and ask her what *she* should do.

"He's good with animals," River said.

"All the Coltons are," she agreed. "It must run in the blood." She wondered what traits her child would inherit from Drake, then realized that hurt too much to think about. "How's Penny? Is her ear okay after the bee sting?"

"Yes." River switched his sea-green gaze to her.

"Are you all right after your wild ride?" he asked in the quiet, thoughtful way he had.

Maya nodded. "No harm done."

Except for what had been done to her heart, she thought before she could block it. Her gaze went to Drake. He looked at home in the saddle. Did he also look that way with a gun in his hand, fighting his way through one hell after another?

Survivor guilt because his twin died? Was that the root of his choosing the most dangerous career available? That would explain the darkness and the sense of sorrow she sometimes detected within him.

At that moment he rode over to the fence. "He's a good mount," he told River. "Rides like a gentleman."

River nodded. "I'll take him now. I think Maya has news for you."

Maya frowned at River, not sure what he meant. He smiled slightly, then dropped to the ground on the other side of the rail and took the horse's reins. Drake vaulted over the fence and stood close to her, waiting, his gaze roaming over her in familiar ways.

"Johnny can come out to the ranch on weekends. You'll have to go over and pick him up."

"Ride with me."

"What?"

"Ride over with me. You know what the kid looks like. He'll probably feel more at ease with you present."

"I'm not supposed to leave the boys."

A sardonic smile touched the corners of his mouth.

"Your teacher friend will be with them for an hour. That's plenty of time."

For what, part of her wanted to ask.

Although his eyes hinted at passion carefully controlled, she really didn't think he was thinking of seduction. Who would, with her present condition? She looked like a blimp. And felt worse. She sighed.

"Back hurting?"

She shook her head.

"Then let's go."

She hesitated. "Let me tell Andy where I'm going. And Mom. She tends to worry about me."

"Don't we all?" Drake remarked softly behind her.

After casting him a quelling glance, she hurried to the kitchen, told her mother of her plans and asked her to tell Andy if he came looking for her. A few minutes later she was sitting in the pickup that Drake had bought and restored years ago. She wondered why he hadn't traded it for a flashy sports car.

"You've been home almost a week, a week tomorrow," she said without thinking.

"Are you wondering when I'll leave?"

"Yes."

He snorted at her stiff reply. "I have a couple of months leave, more if I need it," he said cryptically.

She wondered why he would need more. "You've never stayed more than a week or two in the past."

"I've never had a pregnant woman to deal with before," he said as if this explained everything.

"You don't have one now."

"Oh, yes, I do."

His sudden laughter, soft and sexy, grated over her nerves, and she felt near tears. "Don't."

"You're right. I'm sorry."

She didn't understand any of the nuances between them, the flashes of insight, the longing, the desire. They arrived at the Hopechest Ranch without further conversation. Johnny was waiting on the porch at the office. She greeted him and went inside to sign him out.

Back at the pickup, she realized why she shouldn't have come. Drake shooed her over to the middle so Johnny could get in. He made sure she was buckled in, then spoke to the teenager. Maya introduced them.

"Thanks for having me over," Johnny said, eagerness in his dark eyes. "Sure beats doing chores around here."

"We'll have chores, too," Drake said. "I promised River we'd muck out all the stables this weekend. He's short of help since a couple of his best hands eloped." He chuckled. "It's a hazard of modern times, having to hire both male and female wranglers."

Maya made herself as small as possible on the ride back to the Colton spread, but that didn't stop her from being intensely aware of each lurch of the truck that caused her shoulder or thigh to brush his. His frequent glances told her he felt the heat, too.

She practically pushed Johnny out of the vehicle and into the house when they arrived. After introducing him to her mother, who set him down to a glass of milk and warm cinnamon rolls before he began his studies, Maya took her student to Andy and the boys.

Her nerves settled down as she went over the familiar territory of lesson plans and practice drills. By noon, she felt in control once more.

Until lunch. Drake was in the kitchen when she and Andy entered with their three charges.

"Drake," Teddy shouted, so obviously happy to see his older brother it made Maya ache. "Can we practice roping after lunch? Johnny is going to try it, too, aren't you?" he said to his newfound friend.

"Indoor voice, please," she reminded the youth.

"One hour of roping, then two hours of mucking the stables." Drake grinned, looking so handsome it made the ache surge through Maya again.

Really, she had to get over this roller-coaster emotional thing around Drake. When the baby was born, when she got her degree, when she left, things would be better.

The thought of leaving caused a separate ache all its own. Catching Drake's observant gaze on her, she put on a smile and supervised lunch.

Drake gritted his teeth at the familiar clenching sensation deep inside each time he looked at Maya. He noted her ease with her fellow teacher and the way she avoided looking *his* way. Something hot and angry burned in him.

He wanted to snatch her away from all other males, including the teenager who looked at her with adoration in his eyes and his younger brothers who vied for her attention like two pups wanting to be petted. But most of all, he admitted, he wanted her away from the other adult male who obviously had her complete trust.

Silently, as if he were the outsider in the family, he watched the interactions of the others. The loneliness that was an ingrained part of his life, except for one magic week last summer, flooded through him. It collided with the unexplained anger that roiled through him.

After the meal, the boys dashed outside to set up the sawhorses for targets, talking a mile a minute to their new friend. Drake followed more slowly, aware that Maya and the tutor hardly noticed when he left.

Outside, he breathed deeply and wondered what the hell was wrong with him these days. His life had always been planned and on track. Until his father's letter telling him about Maya and the baby.

Hearing voices, he watched as Maya walked to the car with Andy Martin. Their heads were close together as they discussed their students' progress for the day and made plans for next weekend. Without thinking, he strode closer.

Neither noticed him.

"Let's meet in town Wednesday," Andy proposed. "We can plan a course of study for the boys as well as Johnny."

"Good idea," Maya agreed with a lot more enthusiasm than she'd shown to any of *his* suggestions.

Drake strode forward. "Maybe you'd better select a wedding date while you're so busy planning the future."

The silence was instant and absolute between the other two. Drake heard the prowl of the wind through the cottonwoods, the muted shouts of the boys from the corral, the plangent warning of his own heartbeat, telling him he'd made a terrible mistake. Hell, he'd known that before the words were out of his mouth.

Before he could apologize, Andy stepped in front of Maya. "Maybe you'd better apologize to the lady," he said, "before you eat your teeth."

Drake laughed at the idea of a teacher besting him, a Navy SEAL. "You're going to make me eat my teeth?"

The other man's face flushed deep red. Drake changed his stance as the teacher assumed fighting mode.

He readied himself for a charge, welcoming the demands of a tussle as he calculated his enemy's next move. He needed action, anything but the impasse of trying to talk to the woman whose eyes expressed shock and horror as the fight progressed.

The teacher charged. With a deft move, Drake simply flipped the other man into the dust.

His satisfaction was short-lived as he realized he'd made another tactical error. Maya rushed forward, bending over Andy, her manner one of total sympathy.

"You brute!" She glared up at him.

"I didn't hurt him," he said, obliged to point out this fact when she didn't seem to notice it. "He led the charge."

She straightened and put her hands on her hips. "You provoked it."

She looked so kissable, he nearly grabbed her and laid one on her pursed, disapproving mouth. Heroically, he refrained, another thing she didn't seem to appreciate, in addition to the fact that he hadn't broken her stupid friend's neck.

"Well," he said, stalling for time while he tried to think, "he was touching you."

"Touching me?" she said in exasperation, again not catching on to the finer nuances of the situation. "Oh, for heaven's sake! Just…just get out of my sight."

Drake pulled his dignity around him, her words adding insult to injury as far as he was concerned. He sauntered into the house.

Inez was in the kitchen as he expected. After pouring a cup of coffee, he propped a hip on the stool at the end of the counter and watched her prepare fish for baking. He sighed heavily.

"Problems?" she asked.

Relieved that she always understood a man, he nodded. "Maya," he said, disheartened by his whole visit home. "Nothing is going according to plan."

He'd expected Maya to be grateful to him for returning to see about her, to take care of her so she wouldn't have to worry about the child's future. And this was the thanks he got—her fury.

"I just don't understand her at all," he muttered.

Inez brushed butter over the fish fillets. "Mothers-to-be are unpredictable."

"I'll say," he agreed glumly, still feeling the sting of Maya's calling him a brute.

"Hormones and all, you know. The body changes a lot."

He nodded. Recalling the slender perfection of last summer and comparing it to the rounded curves of the present, he felt the not-so-subtle changes in his own body as heat flowed to that dark place deep inside.

Hunger surged through him, the desire not at all slaked by the changes in Maya. In some ways, she was sexier than ever, the baby proof of the wild passion they had shared, reminding him of the ecstasy he'd tasted with her and no one else. Longing joined the hunger.

"One thing I know about my daughter," Inez continued after a few seconds of silence, "she would not give her body where her heart did not also go."

Misery coiled in his chest, making it tight and achy. "She seems real close to Andy Martin."

"Yes, Andy is her friend." Inez rolled the fillets in cracker crumbs sprinkled with grated cheese, then laid them in a baking dish. "It's wise for lovers to also be friends."

"He isn't her lover," Drake said furiously.

"Someone was."

Heat hit Drake's face as this inescapable truth quivered in the air between them. "I'm sorry," he said. "You're her mother. I shouldn't have…"

"A mother has to let go when her daughter becomes a woman. Still, it isn't easy to stand by silently while your children make mistakes." She gave him a wise but sad smile. "You will learn this with your daughter."

"Marissa. Maya is going to name her Marissa."

"A beautiful name," Inez said in approval.

A fist closed around his heart. He looked at his hand and recalled the baby thumping against his palm as if welcoming him home. His twin's face appeared, and Drake shook his head in confusion. The darkness returned, driving out the warmth and light of passion.

"My work," he said, trying to explain. "It's dangerous. There's no place for a wife and child where I go."

"Woman have gone with their men to dangerous places in all of history," Inez told him in a gently scolding voice. "Perhaps it's your courage that is lacking."

Her dark eyes, so like her daughter's, gazed at him with her usual kindness, yet he felt rebuked. "Someone has to be practical about the situation," he told her as need and hope fought with his conscience.

"I have often found Maya to be levelheaded."

"Maybe," he said doubtfully.

Obviously the mother didn't know her daughter at all. Needing movement, he headed for the corral. Maya was there, sitting on the top rail with no regard for her condition as usual. The familiar anger coursed through him, dislodging the other, confusing emotions.

"Be careful," was all he said, though, as he leaped over the fence to begin the roping lessons.

"I am," she said with no inflection, which told him she was still furious with him.

"You want to try your luck from a horse?" he asked the boys.

Joe and Teddy thought that sounded great. Johnny didn't say anything. Drake studied the teenager while he supervised the saddling of three trusty ponies. Johnny did exactly what Joe and Teddy did, but his fingers were awkward at the task. His mount had to take the bit on its own and practically put its own head in the halter.

"Be sure and loop the reins," Drake instructed the younger boys as he realized Johnny wasn't familiar with horses. He demonstrated and made them retie the leather, then showed them how to mount in one smooth leap.

Johnny followed his every order. Drake nodded approval when the teenager sat in the saddle, his shoulders tense, the reins in one hand the way Drake held his.

"As soon as you lasso the sawhorse, the pony will hold the rope tight. Jump down and keep your hand on the rope as you run to the target to release the rope. Remember, that would be a live, squirming animal on the end if this were real."

Aware of Maya's eyes on him, he gave the kids pointers and watched their skills improve rapidly. Maya was right—Johnny was a quick learner. Maybe the boy could get a sports scholarship to college. He'd talk to Maya about it. That should get her attention.

He broke off that line of reasoning. He wasn't thinking of the teenager's future just to get her approval. Although it did irk him that she refused to even glance his way while she kept an eye on her charges. As if she didn't trust him to watch after them properly.

Later that afternoon, when he went to his room to shower and change for dinner, he considered something that had occurred to him earlier. Maya no longer trusted him.

But he'd told her, in the note he'd left, that his life was too uncertain. He'd said things in passion that he hadn't meant to say, but then he'd explained why he had to leave and why he had to go alone…

Why?

The question ambushed him, bringing him to a stumbling halt, but only for a second. Then reason reasserted itself.

He'd explained it all, dammit. He didn't have a life like normal men. His future was one that couldn't be depended on.

Why?

Because of his missions. His return was never guaranteed. Because he'd vowed to never leave anyone behind to mourn his passing.

The way he'd been left behind when his twin died?

He had no answer for that. It just wasn't fair for a man in his position to have a wife and kids…except there was already a kid on the way. And Maya…

His breath caught at the thought of greeting her warm, sweet welcome with the fierce passion she stirred in him each time he came home, safe and sound, to her arms.

The new scar on his hip throbbed. The problem was that he might not always return. The one left behind suffered in a hell that never let up.

Except for those wild moments of incredible passion last summer.

He shook his head as pain ran over him. He shouldn't have taken her innocence, her trust, nor her love if he hadn't meant to return it.

Emotion he couldn't define plunged wildly through him. He had to go to her, to tell her...what?

A man with no future had no right to involve another in his life. That was what he had to make her see. If that meant she had to turn to another man—

The idea wasn't bearable. He and Maya had to come to terms. Their child's future depended on it. That's what he had to think about—Marissa's future.

Suddenly a whole world of possibilities opened before him.

Seven

Maya hurriedly looked through her notes. Yes, she had everything. Didn't she? She riffled through the papers again. Yes. She had to grin at her nervousness.

Today was the big test, the last of the semester. All her other classes had required a term paper, but not the one on early childhood assessment methods. The prof gave long, hard tests that took three hours.

Closing the folder, she stuck it in the tote bag with a packet of cheese crackers and a bottle of water. She hurried to the kitchen to tell her mom she was on her way. Drake was there.

She nodded to him only because her mother was present. "I'll be home by nine, I should think," she said. "The boys have their instructions and will study here in the kitchen before dinner. Each gets to choose one hour of television, Teddy first this time, then Joe

has to read to you from one of the books on his desk
for thirty minutes.''

"I remember,'' Inez said, stirring a pot on the
stove. "Then I read a chapter of Teddy's book to him.
Joe gets to listen. Both go to bed at nine.''

"Where are you going?'' Drake asked, frowning.

Maya answered reluctantly. "San Francisco.''

"She has an exam,'' Inez added, a worried light in
her eyes as she looked Maya over. "I don't like your
being out on the road alone for such a long time.
There's a storm coming. What if something happens?''

"Nothing will happen,'' Maya assured her mother.

"You could have a flat tire. The road could wash
out. You know we have mud slides at this time of
year. Spend the night in the city if we get rain.''

"Well, we haven't had but one drizzle in a week.
I'll be okay. Stop worrying,'' Maya scolded affectionately.

"Here's your lunch.'' Inez handed her a plastic
bag. "In case something happens and you need to
eat.''

With a resigned smile, Maya tucked the bag into
the tote, gave her mother a kiss and headed out. Drake
rose and followed her. She was as aware of him at
her heels as she would have been if he'd been a wolf
bearing down on her.

At last she turned on him. "What?'' she demanded.

"You going in that old car of yours?''

The question surprised her. "Yes.''

"No way.''

"I beg your pardon?'' she said haughtily.

"I'll take you. Don't argue," he advised. "It won't do you any good."

"I don't need anyone to take me."

"Please."

The softly spoken word hung in the air between them. Perhaps if she hadn't looked into his eyes...but she did. She saw determination, but also worry, and the bleakness that never left him.

"You don't have to," she said, trying to reason with him and her stubborn heart, which pounded eagerly at the thought of hours alone with him.

"I know, but...I'd worry."

The simplicity of the statement undermined her resolve to have as little to do with him as possible.

She went with him, not without misgivings, to his well-maintained truck. Once they were on their way, she sighed and relaxed. "I have to admit, it's nice to be able to watch the scenery instead of the traffic."

His eyes flashed over her. "Yeah."

Heat worked its way through her as Drake guided the pickup onto the winding road over the mountains to Highway 101, which was faster going than via the coast road. Even so, the trip took the rest of the morning. They spoke rarely, but, with soft music on the CD player, the silence eased into a semi-comfortable companionship. It was after eleven when Drake joined the traffic pouring across the Golden Gate Bridge into San Francisco.

The sky was overcast, and a mist fell on the city, driven by a chill wind off the Pacific.

"Let's have lunch at one of the places along Fisherman's Wharf," he suggested.

"I'd rather go to the campus. I want to look over my notes once more," she said.

"Okay. You'll have to direct me."

He expertly followed her orders, and they arrived at the busy university buildings shortly after that. Parking was a problem, as usual, but they finally found a space.

Drake got out and fell into step with her as she headed for a quiet alcove on the first floor of the building where the exam was to be held.

"You'll have hours to kill," she told him. "It'll be four before the exam is over."

"I brought a book to read. Is there a cafeteria or someplace to get lunch?"

She rummaged in the tote and brought out the meal her mother had sent. "Mom sent food in case I was marooned on a deserted island for a week. You want to share?"

"Sure. I'll get drinks," he said, pointing to a machine with a variety of canned sodas in the lobby.

Maya watched him, his stride long and sure, as he bought drinks for them. The misery and excitement of being with him left her confused and wary. She'd been wrong to follow her heart last summer. She wouldn't be foolish again, she vowed, no matter how wonderful Drake could be at times.

He'd been super to Johnny and his younger brothers over the weekend, working with them for hours at the stables. Drake seemed to have a natural affinity for youngsters. He'd been endlessly patient and good-humored at Joe's and Teddy's demands for attention.

His help had given her a break, although she'd been

careful to stay close and keep an eye on the boys so Ms. Meredith wouldn't worry or get upset.

Laying a hand on her abdomen, she found herself wondering, against her better judgment, how he would be as a father. Firm or indulgent? Loving or distant? Would he spoil Marissa when he came in for one of his quick visits, then ignore her the rest of the time?

If they married, would she turn into a nagging wife, hating it when he went off on one of his missions? What if, one day, he didn't return?

She worried about the dark part of his soul that drove him to court danger and challenge death. However, he wasn't a thrill-seeker or adrenaline junkie. Drake had a strong sense of right and wrong. He was an honorable person.

And therein was the problem. He would marry her and try to give her the life he thought she wanted. To make things right—that was his nature and why he'd chosen his life's work. It was also a part of why she loved him.

Longing for more than life seemed to offer seared her with needs she'd suppressed the past few months. Pride had refused to let her contact Drake when she'd realized she was expecting. She'd heard nothing from him after he left.

There's no place in my life for a wife and family.

The stark, written denial of their softly spoken words of love were burned forever into her heart. For a moment, she felt pity for that young, trusting girl who had given her love so freely. It had been a bitter awakening to read that note and know Drake had left—

"Here," Drake said again and handed Maya the soda can and a straw.

He wondered what thoughts had taken her away. Jealousy flamed in him. He wanted her in every way—her thoughts, her time, all her attention. He shook his head as knowledge, bitter and lonely, forced him to remember all the reasons he should leave her alone.

Except it was too late for that.

Looking at her rounded figure, yearning tore at him. He wasn't even sure what he longed for. A return of the raw passion they had shared last summer? Yes. A renewal of the trust in her eyes when she gazed at him? God, yes. Her love?

He'd never allowed himself to think of the softer side of life and the comfort of home and family. Those weren't in the cards for him. That was a fact he'd always known, long before he'd chosen a career or felt this passionate intensity toward Maya. He hadn't meant to hurt her....

But he had.

That was another fact he had to face up to. Years ago, when she'd been seventeen and just blossoming into womanhood, he'd noticed and been attracted. Sense had prevailed, and he'd fled the homestead.

Too bad he hadn't exercised the same caution last June. Now it was too late. He let his gaze wander over her, noting the way her hands trembled as she ate and read over the notes. She'd always hated tests.

It came to him that their lives had been and would

always be entwined in many ways. Whether she agreed or not, he had to think of her and the baby. All his assets were now assigned to her—his insurance, saving account, trust fund—in case he didn't come back from a mission.

He ate a sandwich, carrot sticks and an apple with hardly a notice as worry gnawed at him. In his inner vision, he kept seeing a pair of big, brown eyes, like Maya's, only in a younger face, filled with trust. He wanted to explain about his work and his commitments to this new life, but his excuses seemed feeble and self-serving instead of noble as he'd once thought. Maybe there was room in a life for more than one thing....

Watching Maya, he saw her close her eyes. Her lips moved as she went over some bit of information she wanted to remember. "Give me your notes," he said. "I'll quiz you."

When she handed them over without a quibble, he realized just how worried she was. For the next ninety minutes, he asked questions, all of which she answered perfectly.

"You'll ace the exam," he told her.

"I hope."

He had to smile at her fatalistic tone. She'd always been a serious student, eager to learn. She'd been the same as a lover, eager to please and to explore the full realm of passion with him.

His body went hard with needs long denied but dreamed of nightly. Without thinking, he leaned forward and kissed her soft, soft mouth. "Good luck," he murmured, knowing he had to let her go.

"Thanks."

He watched her gather her composure and the papers, then walk down the hall, joining other students entering the theater-style room. He got out a book on naval maneuvers in past wars and settled down to wait.

After a couple of chapters, he gave up on the book. His mind kept drifting to Maya and the baby and their future. Their daughter would grow up, marry, have children of her own. Would he be around to see it?

Outside, the storm came down in full force, bringing wind and heavy rain. The mountain road would be hazardous.

At three, he called Inez and found out it was raining hard there, too. He made a decision. "I think I'll see about rooms and spend the night in town," he told the housekeeper.

"That's good. I was worried about Maya being out on the road in this storm."

Guilt nibbled at him, but gently, while he made arrangements for two rooms with a hotel down on the bay. It wasn't as if he'd planned the storm or anything. Even her mother had been relieved to know Maya wouldn't be out in the weather. Yes, staying in town was definitely the best thing to do.

Beyond that, he didn't want to think.

Maya handed the test to the student aide at the door and walked out of the room, glad the ordeal was over.

"How'd it go?" Drake asked.

He was leaning against the wall, his hands tucked in his pockets, his stance casual.

"Fine," she said, looking away. "It's raining," she added, as if just noticing this fact.

"Yeah. I talked to Inez. The storm has closed in all along the coast. I, uh, told her we would stay in town for the night."

Maya hugged the tote bag to her chest. "Yes, it would probably be wise."

She knew that was a lie. She wanted it too much. Hours alone with him. The whole enchanted night.

He led the way to the car, pointing out puddles to be avoided, his manner brisk, almost impersonal. But his eyes...they spoke of intimacies once shared, of being in his arms, hidden from reality, just the two of them.

The hotel was near the tourist district with commanding views of the bay, Alcatraz Island and the Golden Gate Bridge, barely visible through the gray sheets of rain. Their rooms were across the hall from each other on the seventeenth floor.

"Is this okay?" Drake asked when they were alone.

She stood at the window and stared at the bay, then the street, crowded with office workers going home, far below. "Yes, it's fine."

He crossed the room and stood behind her. "What do you see that's so interesting?"

"Nothing. Just the street. It looks like a painting, all misty and soft gray, with the bay in the background."

"It'll be deserted soon. The street people and tourists are already gone for the day."

She inhaled deeply, taking his scent into her, feeling his warmth at her shoulder. She wished life was different.

Grow up, she advised. A sigh escaped her.

"Tired?"

His hands went to her shoulders, his fingers like magic on the tense muscles of her neck and upper back. She didn't object. She knew she should, but she didn't.

What did it matter now if he touched her?

That was foolish logic, but at the moment she didn't care. This was Drake, the boy she'd worshipped as a child, the man she'd come to love as only a woman can. Drake, with his sense of responsibility and need to atone for a crime he didn't commit. Drake, so kind to others, so harsh on himself.

She faced him, all her love on the surface. She couldn't hide it from him or herself.

He swallowed hard, then touched her cheek with his fingertips. "I've dreamed of you, of us, alone like this, all those months I was away."

His loneliness was a bleak destiny, a darkness in the golden depths of his eyes. Her heart went out to him.

"We could have been together."

"Sometimes it seems possible."

"But it isn't," she concluded.

"I don't know."

His admission spoke of longing he couldn't hide. The muscles in his jaw moved, and she sensed he was hanging on to his control, but only by a precarious thread. If she pushed ever so little…

"I think I'd like to rest for a while."

He dropped his hand and stepped back. "Of course. Do you want dinner in, or shall we go out?"

The hotel had a restaurant on the highest floor, one of her favorite places to dine. "I love it upstairs. It's like being on top of the world."

"All right. About seven?"

"Yes, that would be fine."

Their formality was somehow ironic, filled with nuances of hunger for other than food. Drake nodded and left.

Maya stood at the window for a few minutes, her eyes on the misty view, her mind oddly empty. It was as if she waited, as if she were expecting something, or someone.

A shudder rippled down her back, and she retreated from the cold seeping through the glass. Lying on the bed, she closed her eyes as weariness crept over her in gentle waves of drowsiness, one after another, until she slept.

The restaurant was surprisingly busy for a rainy Monday night, Maya noted when she and Drake were seated. A large group noisily occupied one side of the room. Fortunately their table was a quiet nook beside a window that overlooked the bay. Streetlights reflected off the wet pavement. Lights from the islands dotting the bay were vague halos in the inky blackness of the night.

"Did you sleep?" Drake asked.

"Yes, soundly. To my surprise."

He nodded. "You were tired. Tests always get you uptight. As if you weren't going to ace them."

She started to protest, but smiled and shrugged instead. "A basic insecurity, I suppose, about being tested and not meeting expectations."

"You've never come up short, as far as I know," he assured her.

His voice was smooth and melodious as usual, but the undertones were deeper, rife with meanings she couldn't decipher. Each time she looked up, his eyes were on her, moving restlessly from her mouth to her eyes and back.

Another couple passed them. The woman was dressed in a smart black pantsuit, her figure sleek and perfect. Maya glanced at her own outfit of navy slacks and the usual tentlike maternity top. She was anything but svelte.

"It's like an island up here," Drake said, switching his attention to the view from the window. "Like being alone in some strange, alien place suspended between the earth and the sky. The cars could be space ships light-years away."

"We're on a space station, circling the universe," she said, joining in the fantasy.

"Yes."

His voice was soft, filled with promises like a warm wind in winter, hinting at springtime.

Inside, she was filled with a sense of urgency, of life pushing at the seams of earth, ready to grow and blossom. After the long winter, she was ready for the fulfillment of promises not spoken, but there nonetheless.

Her composure wobbled. She was glad when their salads arrived and she had something to concentrate on besides him and the arcs of awareness that flowed like electricity between them. After a while, she wished the meal to be over as every moment became a separate, painful wish that it would last forever.

Nothing lasts forever, she told herself, but that didn't stop the wishing.

"You look so solemn. What are you thinking?" he asked, ignoring the steak platter the waiter had delivered.

She cut into the perfectly sautéed fish fillet and considered. "I'm thinking about having one more quarter of tests to go," she said lightly, forcing herself to smile.

"You'll have the baby by then."

The smile melted. "Yes."

"How will you manage?"

"Newborns sleep most of the time. I'll take Marissa to class with me the last month."

"Are you going to breast-feed?"

The oddest sensation speared through her breasts at the question. "I—I thought I would. I mean, it's so much better for the baby."

"Good," he said solemnly.

She made the mistake of looking in his eyes. The stark loneliness she saw there nearly made her weep. Resolutely, she continued eating until the moment passed. At last the meal was finished.

"I think I'd like to go to my room now," she said, refusing dessert.

"The check, please," he said at once.

She was silent while he charged the dinner to his room. In the elevator, on the way to their floor, she slumped against the wall, feeling the weight of responsibility on her shoulders. She had only to say the word and Drake would step in, offering marriage and an easy way out of her worries about making it on her own with a baby.

Pride wouldn't let her consider this solution to her problems for more than a minute. She had made her bed and she would lie in it. Alone.

At her door, she quickly thanked him for the meal and rushed inside, locking the dead bolt behind her. She felt his presence on the other side before he opened the door directly across from hers and quietly closed it.

She breathed easier after that. Besides the standard white terry robe, a nightshirt was laid across the pillow. She also found a toiletries kit in the bathroom.

Knowing Drake had thought of the items for her, she brushed her teeth with the travel-size toothbrush, slipped into the nightshirt and got in bed. With the TV on an old movie, which should have put her to sleep, she lay awake, restless and tense.

Nine o'clock passed. Ten. Eleven.

Sitting up and turning on the lamp, she looked around the room for something to read. She flicked through a magazine extolling the attractions of San Francisco. She glanced at the window where the rain beat in a monotonous drone against the glass. A hotel room in a rain-drenched city was the loneliest place in all creation.

A knock came softly at the door.

"Maya?" Drake said.

She pulled on the robe and opened the door.
"Yes?"

He came inside. "Is your back hurting?"

"Is rain wet?" she retorted with wry humor.

"Lie down. I'll rub it for you."

"Not a good idea, Drake."

He froze, his eyes seeking hers. She gazed at him
in despair and longing, her resolve to go it alone weak
at the moment.

"Maya," he murmured, his tone echoing the hunger that couldn't be denied in either of them. His hand
closed into a fist. "I didn't plan this."

She shook her head helplessly. "It's madness...to
want like this, to need someone who isn't there."

Drake reached for her, needing to erase the pain
from her eyes. He saw more than she wanted him to
see—the stubborn refusal to let herself need anyone,
the courage to face life on her own terms, the tenacity
to keep on...

Her courage humbled him, causing him to question
his own convictions. He knew he shouldn't make
promises. His life was too uncertain for that. Yet,
there was the fact of her, her warmth, her goodness,
her love.

"I can't give you what you need," he told her in
a final attempt at honesty. "I am what I am."

Maya closed the one step that separated them, as
drawn to him as a stray planet captured by the sun.
"You are what I need," she said. "You just don't
know it."

He frowned as if in pain. She slipped her arms
around him and laid her head against his chest. He

hesitated, then his arms enclosed her. She sighed, elated and weary at the same time.

"Make love to me," she said.

"I want to. Desperately."

His brief laughter bitter with self-knowledge, Drake guided her toward the bed. Nothing could make him give up this moment, not even knowing he would face a firing squad when morning came, or worse, his conscience.

When she untied the belt, he removed the robe from her shoulders and tossed it to a chair. The nightshirt brushed the midpoint of her thighs and disguised her pregnancy so that she looked as she had last summer.

His heart beat fast as hunger and longing raged through him. She was the woman of his dreams, and he could no more deny the passion between them than he could willfully stop breathing. It was too much to ask of a man.

"Let me look at you," he requested.

When he gathered the nightshirt into his hands, she didn't protest. He lifted it carefully over her head and laid it aside.

Dropping to his knees, he pressed his cheek to her abdomen and marveled at this evidence of life, this miracle he had helped create.

"Lie down," he said.

Maya stacked the pillows against the headboard and leaned against them, unable to tear her gaze from the man who watched her as he undressed. His gaze seemed lambent in the lamplight, all the tenderness inherent in his nature gathered in those depths.

An arc of golden light flashed through her, leaving an afterglow of trembling anticipation. This was Drake, the man she had loved all her life. Whatever the cost—and it would be high—she would take this night.

When he joined her in bed, she surrendered doubt to the wanton ecstasy of his touch.

"You're beautiful," he murmured after kissing her mouth, then along her neck.

She smiled at the exaggeration, but said nothing.

He took her breasts into his hands. "You're different here, too. Not just bigger, but…"

Her nipples had changed from pale pink to a dusky rose shade. "Darker," she said. "That's natural, I read."

"There's more of a glow, too."

He touched her cheek and trailed a finger down her chest, leaving a molten path along her skin. He laid a hand on her tummy, leaving warmth there, too.

"Can we do this without hurting you?" he asked.

She blinked up at him, then smiled. "Yes. Right up until time—" She stopped as a blush slid into her face.

"I'll be gentle," he promised.

She closed her eyes as need and yearning flamed and grew and entwined. She ran her fingers into his hair and brought his face to hers.

The kiss was sweet at first, before it became desperate. She moved restlessly against him as the passion claimed her. His scent filled her. The masculine feel of him all along her side sent delicious spirals of need shooting off inside her.

"Drake," she whispered as desperation seized her.

His touch became familiar, intimate, arousing. She caressed him the same way, exploring his body as he explored hers, finding all the ways to drive him to passionate insanity. He did the same to her.

"What's this?" she asked, pausing at a raised furrow of flesh she didn't recall.

"Nothing," he murmured, his eyes passionately exciting as he caressed her breasts.

She pushed against his chest until he reluctantly turned and let her see. She gasped when she saw the pink of a new scar along his hip. "You were hurt."

He shrugged. All in a day's work, the gesture implied.

Tears filled her eyes. "On the last mission?"

"Yes." He grinned in a disarming way meant to reassure her. "It didn't slow me down, then or now," he added huskily, his hand caressing along her thigh.

Catching his wandering hand with its magical touch, she brought it to her lips, then pressed her cheek against the palm. "I would hate it if you died. I would grieve forever. In my heart, I would."

His expression hardened. The tension increased. She gazed at him steadily, refusing to be intimidated.

I love you.

The words stuck at the tip of her tongue. She didn't say them, but neither did she try to deny them. This was Drake, the love of her youth, of her woman's heart.

"You don't allow anyone to trespass into your emotional life," she whispered, "but if you accept my body, you must also accept my feelings."

"There's no future in it. I don't—"

She laid her fingers over his lips. "You do have something to offer. Yourself. Just as you are. Not as a hero who will go into any danger in order to save lives, but as a man who is incredibly kind and gentle. I've watched you with the boys. You have so much goodness in you, Drake. Why won't you see it?"

Passion receded and tension escalated. She regretted the admonition as the silence grew longer.

"What you think you see in me is only a pale reflection of what you are," he finally said with an intensity that stilled her protest. "You are the good things...the things I fight for when I go out."

The words seemed pulled from that dark place that lived inside him. She blinked as the tears burned her eyes.

"It doesn't matter," she said, consoling him as best she could. "Only this moment does. Give me tonight, Drake, and let tomorrow take care of itself."

"I can't promise tomorrow."

She shook her head, not wanting to hear it.

He exhaled deeply, then kissed each of her fingertips. "You make me dream, sweet Maya, of things that can never be."

"They can," she said fiercely and hugged him close, as close as possible, wanting to shield him from the pain he would never admit and the need he couldn't entirely deny. "Love me, Drake. Now. I want you now."

He hesitated only an instant, then bent to her mouth with a kiss that reached right to her soul in its loneliness and hunger. She pushed the problems aside and let the desire take her.

"Do I need anything?" he asked.

"Like what?"

He lifted his head, his eyes dark with hunger. "Would you feel more comfortable if I used a condom?"

"Why? I mean, why now?" she asked, perplexed.

He shook his head and caressed her cheek gently. "Such innocence," he murmured. "I'm safe. I haven't been with anyone, not since you."

"Neither have I."

"You didn't have to tell me that. There's never been anyone but me."

She didn't respond.

"Has there?" he demanded gently. He wanted to hear her admit it. He needed the words.

She closed her eyes. "What do you want me to say?"

"Nothing. It's enough that you're here. We have tonight."

For once, he had no plans, no strategy. There was only this moment and this woman. Beyond that, he couldn't think.

He cupped his body around hers, guiding her thighs to rest over his. Then he entered her, finding the ecstasy and the relief from memories that only this woman gave him.

As she cried out and writhed against him, he kissed her as if his life depended on it, as if there would be no tomorrow.

For him, there might not be. He had to remember that one fact. That was the future he had chosen. How could he ask another to share it?

Eight

The rain continued throughout the night and the next morning. Maya had little to say on the trip back to the Hacienda de Alegria, except to reflect that perhaps House of Joy was no longer an appropriate name for the estate.

"It's sad," she began, then stopped.

Drake cast her a thoughtful glance as he drove carefully through the misty gloom. "What is?"

With the dawn, sense had returned and they had retreated from each other and from that place they'd reached during the night, the place where they were both so terribly vulnerable. Making love was only a temporary haven from the reality of life.

"That things have to change. Your parents—" She realized this might not be a good topic.

"I don't think their marriage is very happy right now."

"There's been a lot of stress with the shootings and the kidnapping, then the police investigation."

"Isn't trouble supposed to bring couples closer?"

Maya ignored the cynical undertone. "It can go either way, or so I've read. I think marriage must be hard in the best of times."

He was quiet for a few minutes. "You wouldn't let me say this last night, but I think we should try it."

"Marriage?"

"Yes. For Marissa's sake."

"That isn't fair," she murmured in protest.

"Life never is."

The sardonic resignation in his voice troubled her. "A child needs a stable home. She would sense if we were unhappy. It would confuse her."

"Would we be unhappy? Last night was pretty fantastic."

Sparks shimmered inside her as she relived those moments of magic—his hands, so gentle as he stroked her, his lips, so enticing as he kissed her, his eyes...

Last night there had been moments when she'd felt close to him. With the dawn, the distance had returned. She wondered if he was thinking of his mother and father and the unhappiness that seemed to surround them.

That was the problem when morning came: all the problems came flooding back.

Maya wanted to offer comfort, but she didn't. The complications in their lives seemed insurmountable. She knew she had only to say the word and Drake would make the necessary arrangements; they could be married by noon. And then what? Happily ever after?

Her heart set up a cacophonous beat. They had shared a wild, tender passion during the night. That and a child, were those enough to cement a marriage into one happy whole?

She didn't know, but it was a chance she was reluctant to take. "It's easier to dream of how wonderful it might have been than to know the reality of failure."

"Yes."

He sounded so sad. It broke her heart.

"My parents aren't a good example," he continued. "Yours are. Why does their marriage work? I've never seen Inez or Marco even frown at each other, much less quarrel."

She had to smile. "They do, though. Once Daddy complained about too much spice in the salsa. Mom dumped the entire batch in the garbage. Neither of them spoke during the whole meal. Later, after we went to bed, Lana and I heard them laughing like mad."

Drake's eyes flicked to her. "Sounds as if they kissed and made up," he suggested huskily.

Chills ran along her scalp and down her arms at the look in those golden depths. It was the way he'd studied her last night, as if he wanted to memorize every inch of her.

"Did we do that last night?"

The softly spoken question took her off-guard. "There's nothing to make up."

"I think there is."

"Guilt," she murmured.

"Perhaps." His manner was introspective. "I did leave you to face the music alone—your parents, mine, the town."

"It doesn't matter." She managed a laugh. "One thing I learned is that a person endures. One day at a time."

"Does it ever become easier?" He sounded doubtful.

"Yes," she said, realizing it was true. She studied him, sensing more to the question. "What troubles you, Drake? If it's me, you don't have to worry. I really can make it on my own, even with a baby. I've saved during the past ten years. With very few expenses, I've banked most of what I made. When I get my teaching certificate, I'll have a secure future. I won't be rich, but I'll be able to support Marissa without help."

"What if I want to help?"

"How? By sending money?"

"That's one way," he admitted.

"Money isn't a child's main need."

"I've told you I'm willing to be a full-time parent. And husband."

She swallowed as misery blocked her throat. "Then the baby and I would live with you? Go with you wherever you go?"

"You can't," he began, then stopped, a scowl on his handsome face. "I'm posted to danger zones, sometimes for months on end."

"Don't families ever go to these places?"

"Sometimes, but—"

"But you wouldn't take yours there."

He nodded. "One guy I worked with, his house was blown to bits by terrorists. It isn't a situation I'd recommend for women and children."

"As you said in your note, there's no place for a wife and family in your life," she said, not allowing herself to flinch from the hurtful truth.

He was silent for a mile. "I always thought that, but there's the child to think of."

"Marissa is mine, Drake. Don't try to take her from me. I still have that note. I'll use it in court if I have to."

Instead of anger, his expression changed to one of tenderness. "Mama tiger," he said softly, "I'd never try to take your kitten. As far as I'm concerned, you and Marissa are a package deal."

She wasn't sure what to say to that, so she kept silent and mulled over the conversation. She wondered if she was letting her ego stand in the way. Her mother had cautioned her about excessive pride often during her growing years.

But she wanted so much more than a marriage forced upon them because of the baby. She wanted love and sharing and laughter. Drake saw only the responsibility, but none of the joy of the union. That wasn't enough, not for her, and not for him in the long run.

They arrived at the ranch shortly after eleven, in time to see several people ride off in different directions through the drizzle.

"Something's happened," Drake muttered.

Maya felt it, too. Icy fingers of dread ran along her neck as they went into the house. Joe appeared at the door of his den. "Drake, you're back. Good."

"What's wrong?"

Ms. Meredith appeared from the living room. "Joe Junior has disappeared. He was gone this morning when Inez went to get him up for school."

Her eyes, so like Drake's, flicked to Maya, the anger a palpable force in them, then to her husband. Maya steeled herself for a dressing-down.

"I see no reason to pay someone to watch over the boys if she isn't going to do her job," Meredith said coldly.

"What happened?" Drake interrupted.

Joe returned his wife's frown with one equally ferocious before answering. "He was sent to his room last night for talking at the table."

Meredith glared at her husband for a moment longer, then spun and returned to the living room.

The boys must have been called to the main table for a command performance, Maya surmised, and Joe Junior had gotten in trouble with his mother. She stared out the window at the rain while Drake and his father looked at a map of the area and discussed the areas already searched.

"I think I know where he might have gone," she said.

The men turned to her.

"I showed the boys my old hiding place among the boulders, near the alcove on the beach, recently. A kid can crawl between the boulder shaped like a giant egg and the cliff. There's a clear area under the rocks, roomy enough to sit up and move about. It was my secret castle when I was a child.''

"I'll go look," Drake said at once.

"I'll go, too," she said.

"No," Drake and Joe said together.

"It's too dangerous," Joe continued. "Visibility is nearly zero, and the steps are slippery."

She knew the men were right. She nodded. "Be careful," she said to Drake.

Drake swallowed against the lump that formed in his throat at the worry that darkened her eyes, not just for his little brother, but for him, too.

He'd never wanted anyone to be anxious about him, had never asked for it. With Maya, it wasn't necessary to ask. She was there, like the north star, steadfast in her faith in others. Warmth swept down to that cold dark spot within.

"I will," he said huskily.

He threw on rain gear and headed for the stairs. The mist obscured the beach entirely as he made his way down the steps. Once on the damp sand, he jogged toward the alcove, his eyes on the waves beating against the shore. The storm surge might have reached the rocky area during the night.

With the rain softening the soil, whole hillsides had been known to let go in a mighty rumble and fall like an avalanche on those below.

"Joe," he called when he reached the huge pile of boulders that had once been part of the cliff face.

There was no answer.

Drake lay flat on the sand and, using his elbows, worked his way through the V-shaped opening. Under the boulders was a small room, just as Maya had described. Joe lay on a blanket, curled into a ball, blissfully asleep.

"Hey," Drake said, shaking the boy's shoulder.

"What?" Joe sat up and looked around wildly. "Oh, Drake, it's you," he said in relief.

"Yeah. Time to go home."

Joe shrank back. "I don't want to."

"I know, old man, but you have to face the music sooner or later. Maya's worried about you."

"She should have been home last night," Joe said in accusing tones. His lip trembled and tears filled his eyes.

"She's waiting for you," Drake said kindly. "Come on."

He eased outside and brushed the sand off. Joe followed. Drake laid a hand on the boy's neck. Joe threw his arms around him and held on for a second before screwing up his courage and stepping back.

Drake was surprised at how touched he was by this simple gesture. He'd never been around the youngest kids much, but he felt a bond with them. He thought his own childhood had been happier and easier than theirs, although he couldn't say why. So much seemed to have changed in the past ten years.

The two returned to the house. There their mother—if she was their real mother—grabbed the boy and kissed and cried over him, almost hysterical in her relief.

Drake observed her actions with some concern and a bit of cynicism. Maybe he would ask Maya if she'd read anything about split-personality types. Or he could buy Rand's and Em's evil twin theory. It was beginning to seem plausible.

When Meredith at last let him go, Joe went to Maya. "I'm sorry," he said, misery in the droop of his shoulders.

She brushed the hair off his forehead. "I think you need to apologize to your parents for the worry you caused them," she suggested softly.

Drake smiled slightly when Joe faced the parents. In spite of a skewed family life, Joe and Teddy would be okay, he decided. Because of Maya. She was honest and loving and giving, and they trusted her.

Emptiness grew in him, pushing at the warmth that lingered from the night of passion. A man would miss a woman like her....

"I'm sorry, Mom, Dad," Joe said dutifully.

"You should be," Meredith said, anger surfacing. "That was a thoughtless and stupid thing to do. You worried us half to death."

"I think the boy realizes that," Joe Senior said. "Joe, you'd better go shower, then have lunch. I'll drive you in for the afternoon session at school."

The boy bounded out of the room.

"I'd better go see about him." Maya, too, hurried out.

Drake watched Maya flee. His mother was rather formidable when she got started.

"I have some news from Thaddeus Law," Joe continued to his wife, including Drake with a glance.

"What?" his mother demanded. "Is it about Patsy?"

Joe nodded. "There was a fire at the clinic, set by

one of the inmates. All the records were destroyed. The present head of the clinic wasn't there when Patsy was, but he thought the letter you received was authentic. I suppose we'll have to accept that Patsy is dead and her ashes scattered in the Pacific.''

"She could hardly fake her own death,'' Meredith said as if questioned on the matter.

Drake studied his mother. She was tense. Her eyes, the same color as his, held a feverish glint.

Her manner worried him. Once he'd worked with a guy, a bomb defuser, who had been the soul of quiet competence, then one day the man had exploded in the officer's mess, threatened to blow up everyone and had to be taken away.

The human mind could be a dangerous thing.

His father spoke. "I didn't mean to imply she did. It just makes things a little more complicated.''

"Nothing is complicated! If the police would leave things alone, there would be no problem!''

Puzzled, Drake watched as his mother paced the floor, her hands clenched in rage. He sighed. He no longer understood this woman who had been a tender, nurturing mother in the past. He didn't doubt that her joy had been real when he brought Joe Junior home, but everything after that didn't make sense.

"I'm afraid two shootings and a kidnapping add up to more than a spot of trouble in the eyes of the law,'' Joe said wryly.

With an infuriated little cry, Meredith walked out. Drake listened until the sound of her footsteps was drowned by the slamming of her bedroom door.

His father stared out the window for a few minutes while Drake wondered if he should quietly disappear.

"Thanks for getting Joe," his dad said.

"It was no problem. He was where Maya said."

Joe smiled. "She's good with the boys. How did she do on the test?"

"I'm sure she aced it, but she was nervous. As usual." He shared a smile of understanding with his father.

"Did you two talk about the future?"

"Some. I think we might be close to an agreement."

"A settled life is good for a family. It can bring some of your happiest years."

"Or some of the unhappiest," Drake said, "if the marriage doesn't work."

His father gazed at him, sorrow in his eyes. "Then it can be hell," he agreed.

Patsy deposited the diamond earrings and slammed the lid on her jewelry console. Meredith's jewelry console.

She hated the life she led—Joe, the house far up the coast from the city and any excitement, the housekeeper with her all-seeing eyes. How had Meredith stood it?

Ha! Her goody-goody sister had probably loved it.

Sitting at her desk, Patsy glanced at the bills scornfully. She had more expenses than Joe could possibly know, what with hiring Silas Pike to get rid of Emily, a P.I. searching for the real Meredith and another investigator looking for her beloved daughter Jewel—

lost to her because Ellis Mayfair took the baby away while she slept and wouldn't tell her where he'd hidden the child, which was why she'd had to kill him.

That stupid Pike. He was costing her a bundle. Maybe she could get more money out of Graham. No, probably not. And the ransom money from Emily's supposed kidnapping was useless, marked so that she couldn't use it.

She tapped her nails on the leather pad, then exclaimed in disgust. She needed another trip to San Francisco. Her nails and hair looked terrible, and there was no one competent in Prosperino, no one at all.

If she could find Jewel, she'd take her and the boys to live in Los Angeles. As soon as she inherited Joe's fortune.

He hadn't changed his will. She was sure of that. He'd better not. She needed that money to care for the children.

Her babies. They loved her. Children always loved their mother. Even Meredith's brats loved her, as if she were their real mother.

She laughed in delight. She had them all fooled.

However, Joe was getting harder to handle. It had been a mistake to have Teddy. But how was she to know that Joe had become sterile due to mumps?

However, Teddy had given her a hold over Graham, so that hadn't been all bad. Everything would be fine. She only had to hold on a little longer.

If Pike would hurry up and take care of Emily, if Joe would hurry and meet his end, then all would be well. With a fortune and her adoring children around her, she would be happy. She closed her eyes in ecstasy.

Drake walked aimlessly through the dark. The day had ended on an uneasy note. Dinner had been tense with neither of his parents speaking.

Maya hadn't eaten in the kitchen but had taken dinner for her and the boys to her room. Drake had left her alone, eating in the formal dining room, then leaving the house for a long walk after that. The restlessness was in him again.

He stopped beside the road as he recognized the outline of the country church he had once attended. Changing directions, he went around the church to the small cemetery at the back. Pushing the old wrought-iron gate open, he walked through and stopped.

His heart beat with a dull thud of dread as he contemplated life, a thing he seemed to be doing a lot of lately. Continuing on, he walked past headstones over a century old to the newer section close to the road.

He hadn't been here in years, not since he used to come with his mother to put flowers on the grave stone each Memorial Day. At a small granite marker in the Colton section, he stopped. It was a lonely site with its one child-sized grave.

Michael Colton. Beloved Son and Brother.

His mother had had the last added for him. "Because he knew you loved him," she'd said.

Michael, watch out!

His call hadn't been fast enough to save his twin. His prayers hadn't been enough to breathe life back into that broken, lifeless body lying in the dust. Not enough...

There were some things that could never be made right.

Sitting on a bench, cold with winter dew, Drake rested his forearms on his thighs. A large part of himself was buried here, with the twin he had never stopped missing.

"Michael," he murmured, "there's a child."

He didn't know why he said that or why it felt like a plea. But there was a need inside him that couldn't be denied. He had to find an answer. Or else he thought his soul would die. It had come to that point.

"If you knew Maya... She was only eight when you died. Do you remember her?"

Would Michael love her if he were alive today?

As *he* did?

The question burned down to his soul. "I love her," he said, and that was another pain, one harsher than all the others. More than that, she loved him. And that was the greatest hurt. Because he didn't deserve it. He'd run out on that love, afraid to face what it might mean in his life.

Inez was right. It was his courage, not hers, that was at fault. Because to love was to risk the heart, and that was harder to face than risking his life.

What good did love do? that dark place questioned scornfully, riddling his conscience with the familiar guilt.

It couldn't keep a person from harm or protect them from careless drivers or the other twists that life threw at them. Wouldn't it be better for Maya and the baby for him to stay out of their lives?

A cold, lonely wind swept in from the churning ocean, shaking the trees and moaning around the eaves and spire of the little church.

The yearning churned in him. He understood it now. "I need her," he told the mournful wind. "Living without her is hell."

He tried to be objective, to put longing aside and think of her. Marriage might not be fair. Maybe he was being selfish, thinking of himself instead of her and the child, but the ache grew worse as he thought of leaving them again.

Perhaps if he'd never known her passion or shared those sweet moments in her arms...

But those memories were inside him, too, pushing at those from the distant past, making a place of their own.

He suddenly felt sure, if he missed this chance, there would be no others. The loneliness of his life would be absolute and forever.

He fought the despair, both of the past and that arising from the future. Restless, unable to resolve the many conflicts that raged inside him, he started back to the house.

Inez was in the kitchen when he bounded inside as if running from the proverbial hounds from hell. Or his thoughts, which were the same thing.

"Would you like some warm milk?" she asked. "I'm making a cup for Maya. Her light is on, and I think she sometimes has trouble sleeping. Marco does, too, and milk helps."

The gardener was one of the most patient, peaceful men Drake had ever known. "What bothers his soul? He's the most innocent person I've ever known. One of them," he amended, thinking of Maya.

The housekeeper gave him a fond glance, then poured a cup of milk and set it on the counter next to him. "'For all have sinned and fall short of the glory of God,'" she quoted softly. "We all have our weaknesses. Sometimes we must learn to forgive ourselves. It is perhaps the hardest thing to do. That, and to let the past go."

She smoothed the hair across his forehead much as her daughter had done with Joe earlier. Drake swallowed a lump in his throat along with a sip of warm milk. "What if it's the past that won't let go?"

Inez's long braid, the dark hair mixed liberally with gray, undulated along her back as she shook her head. "We make choices," she advised. "From moment to moment, we decide. Choose your life wisely."

Her smile filled with tenderness, she poured another cup of milk and set it near him, then washed out the pan. "You will take this to Maya when you go to bed?"

Drake nodded, humbled by this woman's kindness and her wisdom...and by her trust. She accepted him as part of Maya's life, knowing that he had been instrumental in the conception of the child, and yet, neither she nor Marco had uttered a word of recrimination when he'd explained his will and the provisions he'd made for their daughter and the coming baby.

Trust was its own burden, he'd discovered long

ago. Michael had followed him across the road, trusting that everything would be fine. Maya had given herself to him, accepting his word that he would take care of her, and look where it had gotten her.

Choices.

He picked up the steaming cup of milk. He knew what he needed to do. Could he convince Maya it was for the best?

Nine

Maya bent forward with a groan. Her back hurt, and the baby was trying some new trick that caused peculiar pains to ripple into her spine. Her due date was the tenth of March, but tonight she wasn't sure she was going to make it.

"Ohh," she gasped as a giant fist pushed against her back from the inside. She placed her hands in the small of her back and tried to equalize the pressure.

Nothing helped.

Knock. Knock.

She grimaced, knowing who was at the door at this hour, which was just short of midnight. Her favorite time of day. She couldn't spare a smile, not even a sardonic one, as the pain eased and she straightened.

"Maya?"

"Come in," she said in resignation. Maybe

Drake's soothing fingers could massage out the ache in her back, although she wasn't sure she could take the strong smell of horse liniment at this moment.

"Your mom sent warm milk," Drake said upon entering. He held the mug out to her.

Maya took it and settled in the rocking chair. Her hand had a slight tremor. "Thanks."

He pulled the desk chair around, sat and crossed his arms over the back, his eyes never leaving her. She found she couldn't smile or put up a false front tonight. The effort was beyond her.

"What's wrong?" he asked.

She shook her head and took a sip of the warm milk, her mother's answer to sleeplessness and other problems. Before she'd hardly had time to swallow, another of the strange gripping sensations started inside.

Setting the cup aside, Maya bent forward as the pressure increased to pain. A low moan forced its way from between her clenched teeth. She held her breath, stopping the sound.

"Maya?" Drake said, his tone sharpening in concern. He rose and clasped her shoulder. "What is it?"

"Don't," she whispered, barely holding on while the pressure grew and grew until it became close to unbearable.

"Is it the baby?" he demanded, letting go and dropping to his haunches before her. "It's the baby, isn't it?"

"Too early," she managed, then inhaled deeply as the pain suddenly let go, as if a belt being twisted around her had broken. She breathed quickly, catching her breath as the strange episode passed. "It's too early. I have twenty-four days to go."

His smile was disarming. "I've heard babies don't pay much attention to schedules and things like that."

"I've had this before. Something like it," she corrected. Nothing had been this severe. "False labor."

"Oh." He returned to the straight-back chair. "Is there anything I can do? You want a rubdown?"

"Not tonight."

She ignored the restlessness, the nervy agitation that made her want to pace, and took several big drinks of milk. That had always soothed her in the past.

But not this time.

Again a gasp escaped her as the squeezing started again, harder this time…lower…faster, as if the thing pushing at her was impatient….

Drake dropped to his knees in front of her and took her hands. "Hold on," he said, his eyes dark in the lamplight.

She nodded, unable to do anything else at the moment. "Uhh," she moaned, then caught her breath as the fist closed hard and pulled her down…down… down…

Closing her eyes, she held on to Drake's hands as the world clamped down to this one place, this moment.

"Ah," she said as the pain stopped abruptly, leaving only the ping, ping, ping of familiar pain in her lower back. She panted and laid her head against the chair cushion. A sheen of sweat broke out all over her. "So odd," she murmured.

"Wait."

She heard Drake rise. He removed his hands from hers and walked away. In a moment she heard the faucet running in the bathroom, then he was back, pressing a cool cloth to her forehead and wiping her face.

Taking the washcloth, she ran it along her throat and around the back of her neck.

"How long does this false labor usually last?" he asked, pulling the desk chair forward so that he could sit directly in front of her, her knees tucked between his.

"I don't know." She wiped her hands on the cloth, then held it while she rested, an odd alertness in her body, as if she waited...

Minutes ticked off. Five, four, three, two...

The next contraction started. She leaned forward, clutching the damp terry-cloth with both hands. Drake's hands closed over hers.

"Easy," he murmured, "easy now, darling."

"Can't," she said. "Too late."

Together, they waited out the gripping pressure that rode roughshod over her will, wresting control from her so that she gasped aloud, then panted and rocked back and forth, wanting it to be done, to release her.

"Drake?"

"Yes?"

"Would you...get my mother? Please."

"In a minute, when it eases."

While she struggled with the pain, Drake mopped her brow, then his own with the washcloth. "You think it's time?'' he asked quietly when she finally relaxed and inhaled deeply.

She looked pale and exhausted. Alarm beat through him. This was beyond his training and expertise. He was afraid to leave her, afraid to stay. She needed help.

''Perhaps I should call for an ambulance—''

''Get my mother, *please*.'' She cast him a pleading glance. ''Ohh,'' she moaned and clutched her knees, bending forward as the labor, false or not, continued.

He dashed out of the room, down the hall and out of the house. Halfway to the housekeeper's neat house set back from the driveway, he realized he should have called.

Cursing, he sprinted faster. At the house, he pounded on the locked door and yelled for the housekeeper at the top of his lungs. A light snapped on inside. Both Inez and Marco appeared at the door, Marco with a shotgun in hand. Drake didn't blame him. He'd have done the same if some madman came shouting in the middle of the night.

''Is it Maya?'' Inez asked at once.

Drake nodded. ''She's in pain, but she says it's false labor. She wants you.''

''Let me get some shoes.''

The housekeeper disappeared. Marco returned the gun to its rack over the fireplace.

''I didn't think that gun worked,'' Drake said inanely.

''It doesn't. I grabbed the first thing that came to hand,'' the older man explained with a sheepish smile. ''I didn't know what was happening.''

"Yeah, well...sorry about waking you and all," Drake finished, feeling foolish. "I was worried."

"Go back to her. Mama and I will be along in a moment."

Drake nodded and dashed back toward the main house. Other than spotlights along the walkway and artfully placed among the shrubbery, plus the night light in the kitchen, only one light shone in the house. He headed for the north wing and the woman he'd left there.

He saw she was having another contraction when he entered. He went to her and took her hands. She grabbed on to him, her grip surprisingly strong while she emitted another of the almost soundless groans that shuddered all the way through him.

Maya was in pain; he was the cause.

That knowledge grated through his conscience as pain also racked through him. He felt helpless and frustrated at the fact. "How can I help?" he asked.

"Let me...hold on," she managed.

He heard the sound of a vehicle, then Inez's voice in the hall. Relief shot through him. The contraction eased, and along with it, Maya's grip. Drake moved aside when her mother entered the room.

"*La niña?*" Inez said.

"*Sí,*" Maya answered. She no longer denied the possibility that this was the real thing. Early or not, the baby seemed intent on coming tonight!

"We need to get you to the hospital," her mother said.

"No time. It's coming."

"Now?" Drake asked, his worry increasing.

"*Sí.* Yes," she said, realizing she was talking to Drake rather than her mom. She looked at her mother. "I'm sorry."

"No need to be," her mother said briskly. "Women have been having babies for centuries. Drake, please call for the ambulance. Marco, you will find an iron in the kitchen closet," she said to her husband, who lingered anxiously at the door. "Please bring it—the heat will sterilize the sheets."

Drake made the call. "Now what?" he asked Inez.

"You must help her to bed. Take off your shoes and get on the bed, too."

Maya was shocked by this order. "Mama," she said.

"You will need the support," Inez explained. She directed Maya to the bed and Drake to get on his knees behind her while she placed a square of plastic and several towels into position. "Let her hold your hands."

Drake wrapped his arms around Maya and let her take his hands. He was startled, then shocked, as he felt something like a wave pass through her abdomen, making it hard...harder...

"Pant," Inez advised. "Scream if you want. It is nothing to be ashamed of. Bringing babies into the world is very hard work."

"I'm okay," Maya said, breathing hard.

Behind her, she felt Drake panting, too. His body was solid against hers, his arms strong as he held her in a half-sitting position.

"You are doing well," Inez assured her. "Ah, the water. Not long now."

Maya could only go along with events as nature took over completely. She panted. Sometimes she ground her teeth together. She moaned. Unable to stop, she pushed whenever her body demanded it.

Behind her, Drake helped her through each contraction as they grew harder and the time between them shorter and shorter until there was nothing but progressive waves of effort…effort such as he'd never seen.

"It's coming," Inez said softly. "Just a little more," she encouraged.

Drake panted with Maya. He held his breath when she did. His own muscles contracted each time he felt her bear down. The worry subsided as he worked with Maya to bring the new life into the world.

"Now, a hard push," Inez said.

And, with an indignant howl, their daughter slipped into her grandmother's waiting hands. Capable hands, thank heavens. Drake let out a great breath of relief.

"We did it," he said softly to Maya, kissing her damp temple as she rested against him.

Her smile was both weary and triumphant.

"Now then, little one," Inez said, giving the baby a vigorous rubdown with a towel. Finished, she held the baby out to Drake. "Say hello to your daddy."

Drake, realizing he was supposed to take the little bundle, sat on the side of the bed. He crooked his arms and Inez laid Marissa into the cradle thus formed. He stared down into the baby's blue eyes.

Her cries stopped. She stared back at him.

"Once more," Inez said to Maya. "Then you can

sleep. Why don't you rock the wee one?'' she suggested to him.

Drake moved to the rocking chair while the birthing process was completed. Inez removed the used towels and the square of plastic from the room, then helped Maya wash and change to a fresh gown. Finally she brushed her daughter's hair and clipped it back at the temples.

''Drake, bring your daughter over to meet her mother,'' Inez suggested. ''You might want to stay and care for the baby while Maya sleeps.''

He nodded and took a seat on the bed. Laying the baby in Maya's arms, he felt a squeezing sensation in his chest.

The child had a crown of black hair that stuck up on her head in an endearing but comical manner. He knew, when she grew older, it would be exactly like her mother's.

Marissa would undoubtedly have brown eyes. Would there also be gold flecks in them like his, or would she have the deeply brown eyes of her mother?

The squeezing sensation became painful as he gazed at his daughter. She was so tiny, so trusting.

Trust. It was a scary thing. So many things could go wrong. For a second, he wanted to run, to get out of the room and away from these women and their belief in life, that it would be fair, that it would work out, that it was okay to bring a new life into the world because tomorrow the world would still be there.

But there was no place to run to, he realized. For ten years he'd traveled all over the world. The past always went with him.

Choices? What choices did he have? The past wouldn't leave him alone. He couldn't change it, atone for it.

Inez finished straightening the bedroom and left. In the hall, he heard her speak to her husband who reported he couldn't find the iron. She told him it was no longer needed and that he had a granddaughter, whom he could see tomorrow. Their voices faded as they walked down the hall.

Maya uncovered the infant and checked her over. "Would you bring a diaper? They're in the last drawer of the chest." She sighed. "Isn't she beautiful?"

"Yes," he said, shaking the pain, feeling humble and somehow proud, as if he and Maya had accomplished a miracle.

He watched Maya diaper the baby, then he put a gown with a drawstring bottom on her while Maya directed, his hands awkward at the task. The baby didn't seem to mind.

"Our daughter," he said with a catch in his voice, looking into Maya's eyes.

He saw her take a deep breath, then she nodded. "Yes, ours," she murmured, acknowledging him as the father.

A funny feeling came from deep inside him, bubbling up to the surface like a fresh water spring pushing its way out of the earth. *Ours.* It was a word that spun visions of the future into his head, like cotton candy growing on its paper cone. He wanted that sweet promise.

"The bassinet is in the closet," Maya informed him. "It's ready for her. I think she's asleep."

He found the little bed and wheeled it over. Maya put the baby down and covered her with a pink and white blanket, then she tucked a rose-embroidered comforter over that. Drake had never seen anything so perfect as their tiny daughter sleeping in her tiny bed.

"It brings a lump to the throat," he said huskily. "This new little being."

Maya flashed him a pleased smile. She patted back a yawn and settled against the pillow. He watched her for a few minutes, knowing she needed rest. She was vulnerable at this moment as she might never be again.

He touched her cheek. "Will you marry me?" he asked.

Her nearly closed eyes snapped open. She studied him before she spoke. "For the baby's sake?"

"For all our sakes. We created this life together. She needs both of us. And I need you…both of you."

He waited out the silence, which seemed more fraught with danger than a stand-off at a shooting match.

Slowly, her eyes on his, she nodded. "It—it seems the right thing."

"It is," he agreed quickly. "This will be right for Marissa. And for us."

He would be the best husband and father anyone ever had, he vowed. He would atone for leaving her when she'd needed him the most. He returned her questioning stare with a level gaze.

She pressed her lips together for an instant, then, "We'd better think about it," she said. "Things might seem different when morning comes."

Seeing the worry in her beautiful brown eyes, he didn't push. Instead he raised her hand and kissed the back of it. "We'll work it out. Let's take each day as it comes. Sleep now. Our daughter will need you fresh and rested tomorrow."

He settled in the rocking chair, his feet propped on the bed while he watched his child and her mother sleep. At the moment, life seemed filled with possibilities and endlessly precious to him. It was an odd feeling, one he couldn't recall experiencing in a long, long time.

A baby. It made a difference in one's life. From a distance, he heard the siren of the approaching ambulance.

Maya woke with a start to a strange sound. She immediately knew what it was.

The baby!

She sat up as Drake lifted the child and smiled at her. "Hi, Mom," he said cheerfully. "I think this girl is hungry. The nurse brought a bottle of warm water, but we couldn't get Marissa to drink it. She has a mind of her own."

"Is she all right?"

"Yep. You need to go to the bathroom or anything first?"

Maya nodded and shuffled across the room. She washed up quickly, anxious to get back to the baby, who was crying. Drake was pacing the floor with her when Maya returned. She was in a private room at the hospital. She and the baby had been checked thoroughly upon admittance and declared "in fine shape," by the doctor on duty.

Sitting in a rocking chair, she held out her arms. Drake handed over the child. Maya unbuttoned her top and the nursing bra, then rubbed the baby's mouth against her nipple as she'd been taught in child care classes. A squeezing sensation pulsed through her breasts.

Marissa bobbed her little head around excitedly. She made funny motions with her mouth.

"You've got to latch on first," Drake advised the baby, laughter in his voice.

Maya continued to work with the baby until, at last, Marissa caught on and began sucking vigorously.

"Aah," Drake murmured, looking supremely satisfied.

When Maya's eyes met his, they both smiled. It was a moment of triumph, a sharing moment.

A worry she hadn't been fully aware of shifted inside her, becoming lighter. She sighed and relaxed as her first experience as a parent became easier.

Drake went to have breakfast after Maya had hers. He was back in the room within thirty minutes.

A new nurse came in later that morning. "Well, here's our big girl. Six pounds-eleven ounces, nineteen inches," she said approvingly. "Has she had anything to eat?"

"Yes," Drake said.

The nurse looked from him to Maya, then back. Her eyes sparkled, but she nodded solemnly. After taking Maya's temperature, blood pressure and vital signs, then the baby's, she wrote on the chart.

The family doctor came in an hour after that. "The impatient ones," he exclaimed, smiling at Maya, then taking the baby. He glanced at Drake, smiled and nodded. "Drake, how ya doing? Still in the SEALs?"

"Yeah. For now."

Drake was aware of the quick glance Maya cast in his direction, but there was no time to explain. He waited silently while the doctor checked out Maya and the baby, then pronounced them both fit to go home.

"Let's get the forms filled out," the doctor said upon finishing. He filled in the birth information. "Baby's name?" He glanced at Drake, then back to Maya.

"Marissa Joy…" Her voice trailed off.

"Colton," Drake said firmly. "Marissa Joy Colton."

He couldn't stop the swell of pride that rushed through him any more than Maya could stop the blush that swept into her cheeks when he claimed the baby as his.

His.

The knowledge gave him a feeling such as he'd never known. That he and Maya had created this tiny life seemed like a miracle. It was something to think about, a future to plan.

Shortly after noon, they left the hospital. Drake steered her into a nearby coffee shop and bakery.

"We'll each have soup and salad and an apple fritter," he ordered, recalling those were Maya's favorite when they'd stopped here last summer. "Mm, better bring two glasses of milk, too."

"Maya, is this your baby?" the waitress demanded, peering at the baby when he placed the infant carrier in a chair between him and Maya.

"Yes."

"Ohh, can I see her?"

"Sure, but don't pick her up. She's too young to be handled yet."

"Of course. Margaret, come see what Maya has," she called to another woman, who came out of the bakery kitchen wiping her floury hands on a towel. "What's her name?"

"Marissa Joy."

"Now isn't that the sweetest thing?" the older woman gushed, peering at the bundle in the carrier. "She's so tiny. How old is she?"

"A bit over twelve hours," Drake told them, unable to contain the ring of pride in his voice.

"Oh, my, brand-new and so sweet." The older woman eyed him. "Drake Colton, isn't it?"

"Yes."

The woman looked him over, then studied the baby. He tensed for more questions, but she only smiled in the knowing way women did when they figured something out concerning a man and his love life.

Again Maya's face went pink. He smiled tenderly. If she hadn't been so stubborn, they could have told these women they were married and legit and all that.

Funny, but he felt married. After all, he was a father, and he and Maya were husband and wife in all but name. They would change that as soon as he could arrange it.

"I came home on leave to welcome my daughter," he said, making his place in this particular scheme of things clear. "And to marry her mother as soon as we can arrange it."

"Oh," both women said, their eyes going wide.

He smiled broadly, enjoying their surprise. Glancing at Maya, he saw she looked thoughtful. He suddenly wished she were happy. He wanted that for her.

It wasn't until they were on the road out of town that he asked, "What troubles you?"

"You," she admitted after a brief silence. "At the hospital, when the doctor asked if you were still in the SEALs, you said 'for now.' What did you mean?"

"I plan on resigning my commission when I finish my present tour of duty."

She looked shocked. "No."

"Yes," he corrected gently, smiling as he contemplated her delight. "As a married man, I need a regular job so I can come home to my family every night."

She shook her head. "No," she said, sounding panicky. "No, it would never work."

"Of course it will." He tried to figure out what she was worried about. "Don't worry. I'll be able to pay the bills. There's a company in Silicon Valley that's offered me a position several times—"

"No!" she said vehemently. "I won't marry you, not like that."

"Why?" he asked, controlling his temper with an effort.

"Because you'd hate it. You'd be miserable. And so would I."

"I see." He swallowed hard as the truth came out. Maya hated the idea of marriage…to him.

So he'd been wrong. They'd shared passion, they'd made a child, but love didn't figure into it.

Stunned, he drove the rest of the way to the house in silence. The loneliness shimmered like a veiled curtain before him, beckoning darkly toward a future he was more and more certain he didn't want.

But it was the one he deserved.

Ten

"She's as beautiful as her mother," Joe Colton said, holding his three-day old granddaughter in his arms. He settled in an easy chair across from Sophie, whose baby was due shortly. Marissa, by coming early, was the first Colton grandchild by blood. Rand had a step-son due to his marriage to Lucy, so now there was Max and Marissa.

"Grandchildren," he continued in an introspective manner. "Wonderful babies to romp through the house and our hearts and grow into flowers as lovely as the roses."

Maya caught the glimmer of tears in the older man's eyes. Glancing at Sophie, Maya realized, not for the first time, that the Colton daughter and River James, a foster child, had also engaged in moonlight trysts last June.

She longed to talk to Sophie, but, even though there wasn't much difference in their ages, Maya had kept her distance from the Colton girls, especially after she started baby-sitting the two youngest boys. Ms. Meredith had made it clear she expected Maya to be available as a servant, not as a companion to her daughters. This fact had always made Maya hesitant to express friendship.

She had always loved Drake and Michael because they had often included all the younger children in their games. And later, there had been the undeniable attraction between her and Drake, first when she was seventeen and he was home from his last year at college, then again last summer.

Last summer. What a time that had been—filled with danger and excitement and the heady experience of falling in love, really in love, for the first time.

She swallowed as the memory became painful. What with Joe Senior getting shot at, it had been a perilous time for all, including the housekeeper's daughter, she reflected with hard-won composure. And now she was the mother of the first Colton grandchild. Marissa slept blissfully in her grandfather's arms, just as she had yesterday with her other grandparents. This was a tangled web, indeed.

The three adults and the baby were in the sunroom, which was warm and cheerful, although the February sun shone weakly through the clouds that gathered along the Pacific coast. Rain was predicted by nightfall.

Drake and River were tending a sick horse, which

might have to be put down. Birth and death, the endless cycle. It made her feel infinitely sad.

"The little darlings may be roses, but parents certainly get a feel for the thorns when they keep waking you up every two hours during the night," Sophie said with an indulgent laugh. "And this is before she's even born."

"Payback time for all the nights you kept your mother and me awake," her father informed her.

Sophie wrinkled her nose at her dad.

Maya closed her eyes as longing rolled over her. She wanted to be like Sophie and River, in love, married and true partners as they planned their lives together.

She and Drake had parted on a tense note when they'd returned to the house. He insisted on marriage, but she knew his heart wasn't in it. That was what hurt. And why she'd had to finally refuse the offer.

Instead of making a place in his life for a wife and child, he was throwing over his chosen path for one he'd decided was best for them. He hadn't discussed it with her. He'd simply made the decision. That wasn't sharing.

Marriage was a series of compromises. No one person could or should give his or her all. Each person needed to contribute to it and to receive due consideration in return. Drake obviously hadn't the slightest notion of those basic concepts in human relations.

She sighed.

"Tired?" Joe asked. "Stretch out and go to sleep, if you like. I'll handle the little one."

"Get as much rest as you can," Sophie advised.

"It may be the last you'll see for the next eighteen years. River is already worrying about curfews and dating and things like that."

This news drew laughter from Joe and Maya. River and Drake entered the room in time to hear it.

"What's so funny?" Drake demanded. He sat on the sofa beside Maya and stretched his arm along the back, not touching her shoulder, but close enough that she felt the warmth from him.

"We were discussing curfews for our girls when they start dating," Sophie explained.

"Marissa isn't dating until she's twenty-one," he declared firmly, eliciting another laugh.

"I'm with you," River agreed. "I'd never sleep if our girl was out after dark with some guy I didn't know thoroughly."

Sophie rolled her eyes. "Next thing we know, they'll be arranging marriages for the babies," she told Maya.

"Probably," Maya agreed.

When she looked at Drake, he was watching her, his eyes narrowed in speculation. He probed deeply, holding her in his spell while he searched for answers to questions she didn't understand. He seemed quiet, pensive rather than angry as he'd been since Marissa's birth. She wished she knew what to do about the tangle her life had become.

"I think I'll go to my room for a while," she said, rising abruptly as the yearning grew stronger.

Taking the baby from Joe, she fled the family scene, feeling very much out of it. She'd hardly gotten in her quarters when Drake knocked on the door, then came in, bringing the bassinet with him.

"You forgot this in your rush to get out of the same room with me."

His expression was impassive, at odds with the pain the words should have conveyed, while he positioned the bassinet near Maya's bed.

"Thanks." Maya changed the baby's diaper, then settled in the rocker for a feeding. She studied Drake, who stood by the window, gazing at the cloud-topped mountains.

"I wasn't rushing to get out of the room because you were there," she said softly, deciding that honesty was the best way to deal with the situation. "It was my own feelings I was running from."

He turned to her without speaking, his eyes flashing golden in the lamp she'd turned on to dispel the gloom.

"I realized how nice it would be if, like your sister and River, we were a real family."

"We could be," he reminded her with a bitter undertone.

She sighed and rocked gently as the baby nursed rather noisily, then tapered off and fell asleep still holding on. When she lost the nipple, she roused and sucked again.

Maya, glancing up, saw pain on Drake's face as he watched her and their child. Her heart contracted into a hard ball of regret. "Drake," she whispered.

"Don't," he said in a rough growl. "I don't want your pity."

"Would you accept my love?"

The words dropped into the abyss between them, as stark as the pain, as challenging as a duel.

"Are you offering it?"

"Always," she said. "I've loved you ever since I can remember."

"Then why—" He stopped, as if to go on would betray some part of him he couldn't disclose.

"Why not accept marriage?"

"Yes."

She met the haunted look in his eyes levelly. "Because my love isn't enough by itself. I want yours in return. I won't share you with Michael."

His head snapped up. Shock, then anger, raced across his face before all emotion was masked behind his iron control. "What the hell does that mean?"

"It means I won't share you with the past." She drew a steadying breath, knowing they were on dangerous ground. He would understand or he would close her out. It was that simple...and that complicated.

He gave a dry bark of laughter. "We're all made up of memories and experience. It can hardly be dismissed."

"But part of you lives in the past you shared with your twin, in those final moments when he died and you decided it was your fault. Do you realize how disrespectful that is? As if Michael had no will of his own."

Maya continued rocking the baby as if she were having an ordinary conversation about ordinary subjects. She knew she was taking a chance that Drake would walk out forever, but the risk was worth it.

"He followed me," Drake said, so low she could hardly hear the words. "I called him a chicken. He crossed the road because of me."

"As you would have done had it been the other way around," she reminded him gently. "You were children, you and Michael. You thought and acted like children. Can't you forgive a child that makes a mistake?"

His hands knotted into fists. Bitterness was etched sharply on his handsome features. "You don't know how it is to live with regret, to know what you cost your family in grief, to face the loneliness of half a life and know it's your fault."

She could have wept for him, but held the tears inside. "I want the whole man, Drake. Not your soul, but your love, freely acknowledged and joyfully shared with me and our child. We deserve no less."

"I'll give you what I can," he promised hoarsely.

She nearly succumbed to the haunted look in his eyes, but she was fighting for their future. "I won't take scraps. It's all or nothing, my love. You can have me and Marissa and the future—or you can have Michael and a past filled with guilt and regrets." She took a deep breath. "It's up to you."

He was breathing fast, as if he'd been running. But Maya knew he could never outrun his past. He had to learn to deal with it. Was she asking too much?

"I don't know how to let go," he told her grimly. "Tell me. If you're so smart, then tell me."

Shaking her head, she admitted she couldn't.

"You're like that damned child psychologist I saw. You think you have all the answers, but you don't.

Because you don't know. You've never lived through it."

He headed for the door.

"I loved Michael, too," she said to his back. "I think he would have adored our daughter."

Drake froze for an instant, then he walked out, closing the door with deadly quiet behind him.

Helpless, Maya rocked back and forth, back and forth, while the baby slept in her arms. She wondered if she was making a serious mistake in not taking Drake as he was.

There was the baby to think of. Every child needed a full-time father. Perhaps she should marry him, then try to reach the hidden parts of him, to win him with her love.

But somehow, she felt sure this was something Drake had to do on his own. If they were to have a real marriage.

She realized she was gambling with their future as much as Drake did each time he went out on a mission. "He must come to us," she resolutely told the baby and held the terrible, terrible grief at bay with an effort.

The ringing of the telephone jarred her. She answered reluctantly, still lost in sadness.

"Maya, this is your big sister. Were you ever planning on telling me I am now an aunt?"

"I meant to call, but...I'm sorry."

"Hey, it's okay. So how's our girl?"

"Fine. An angel. And beautiful."

"Of course. She has designer genes," Lana teased, then sobered. "How is Drake handling things?"

Maya couldn't hold back a sigh. "He thinks we should marry." She explained everything that had happened.

Lana was silent until she finished, then she, too, sighed. "I'll be home soon. My job here is nearly done. My patient is settling in nicely with her sister. Her daughter lives nearby. The Homecare nurse comes by everyday. I'll be coming back to Prosperino soon. Call me whenever you need to. Promise?"

"I promise." Maya said goodbye and hung up. She felt utterly alone for a moment. Then her daughter made a little smacking sound. She smiled, comforted by this small thing.

Drake woke with a jerk from a nap. He'd been dreaming, but he couldn't recall the dream. He didn't want to. His dreams were all nightmares, anyway.

Rising from his bed, he headed for the living room. No one there. His father wasn't in the den, either. From the sunroom, he caught sight of Joe Senior outside, working on the fountain in the middle of the patio garden.

He pulled on a jacket and went outside to help. "Is it broken?" he asked when he was close.

His father glanced up with a start, then smiled in welcome. Drake wondered what the older man's thoughts were.

Family problems, he answered his own question. Trouble was reflected in the blue depths of his father's eyes. Looking into them was like looking into his own soul. Both he and his father were haunted, it seemed, by the past and the present.

"No, no," Joe said. "I'm just puttering. It's what old men do, you know."

"Ah, so that's what I have to look forward to in my dotage," Drake teased.

He picked up the net and dipped some leaves out of the crystal water. His father cleared the spigot where the water usually bubbled. Drake cleaned the filter basket.

"Ready to turn the water on?" Joe asked.

Drake replaced the basket. "Yes."

The water gurgled, shot a spray up in a graceful arc, then plummeted into the circular pool where goldfish swished their tails and swam lazily through the icy-cold, spring-fed water.

"Getting colder," Joe said. "It's supposed to rain tonight." He scanned the sky and the clouds that darkened as the day lengthened into late afternoon.

"Yes," Drake said absently, his mind on Maya and the baby and the changes that a moment of unguarded passion could make in a life.

Lives, he corrected. More than one life was involved in the present conundrum. His. Maya's. Marissa's. Even his mother and father were involved. After all, Marissa was their grandchild. He sighed, frustrated because he was unable to think through the situation and come up with a game plan. Maya wasn't playing along with him, he admitted with a sardonic twist.

Joe sat on the edge of the fountain. Drake propped a foot on it and frowned at the misty ocean.

"I'm adding a codicil to my will," his father announced. "To include your Marissa."

"You don't have to," Drake told him. "I've arranged for everything I have to go to Maya. She and the baby will be taken care of."

"I know you'll take care of your own. This is something I want to do. Your mother and I," he added quickly.

Drake didn't say anything to this last. He wasn't sure his mother would ever acknowledge Marissa. She hardly seemed to know her own children were alive. Except for her on-and-off attention to Joe Junior and Teddy.

"We were so thrilled when you and Michael were born," Joe continued, obviously lost in his own thoughts of the past. "Such beautiful babies. And smart, too. Rand was a toddler then, full of spunk and curiosity. We were so proud of our little family. When Sophie and Amber came along, we thought it was perfect."

"Then the kids grow up," Drake remarked dryly, noting the sadness that flashed through his father's eyes.

Joe nodded absently. "Life moves along, not always down the road you'd prefer it take."

"True. Maya isn't cooperating at all."

Joe studied his son, seeing beneath the surface irony to the man inside, and beyond the man, to the boy who had lived with guilt and regret most of his life. Drake had been the most serious of his children, taking more than his share of responsibility for the family and its welfare. The tragedy of his twin's death weighed on his soul.

"We can't make others conform to our wills," he said, his thoughts going to the Meredith he'd known in the past, unable to keep from comparing her to the present woman who lived in his house but was a stranger to him.

"I don't expect Maya to conform, but we have a child to think of. I don't want to be an absent father."

"A child needs both its parents."

"Yes, but when I told Maya I was going to resign my commission and take a regular job, she got furious about it. She said I decided without consulting her."

Joe suppressed a smile. Drake was frustrated in his attempts to do the right thing, but, man-like, he thought he could decide what was best and follow through. "I take it that Maya has her own thoughts about marriage and the running of it."

"She's stubborn," Drake admitted. "I never suspected how much."

This time Joe did smile. "I remember a quarrel your mother and I had during the early years. I sent you boys to bed without supper for some infraction. She didn't think withholding food was right."

"What happened?"

"No supper was served that night."

"Not to anyone?"

"No one. She said food, like love, was a basic necessity. If part of the family was deprived, then all had to share in the sacrifice."

"I remember that," Drake said, his eyes going

warm with the memory. "We all ended up having supper in the kitchen."

"Right. Your mom and I caught each other sneaking food to you boys, so we joined forces and had an impromptu midnight run on the pantry."

Joe was relieved to hear Drake's chuckle. This trip so far hadn't resulted in the happiness for his son that Joe had expected. His chest contracted in worry. That was the one thing he wanted most of all—a full and happy life for his children. So far Rand and Sophie were the only two who had settled into married bliss.

But then marriage wasn't always blissful.

He had thought often on the moment when his had gone wrong. Was it when Meredith announced she was pregnant with Teddy? No, before that, obviously, since she'd taken a lover. A picture of Teddy's blue eyes and blond curls leaped into his mind along with one of Graham's identical coloring.

He swallowed hard. Surely Meredith, his beloved Meredith, hadn't gone to his brother....

But there had been someone. Betrayal. That was a fact he'd had to learn to live with.

"A man has to learn to put hurtful things behind him," he said to Drake. "You'll have to forgive Maya for not contacting you. Sometimes a person's pride gets in the way of happiness," he suggested, trying to be helpful without putting in his own two cents worth.

"It isn't that. She says I'm living in the past, but I'm trying to think of the future, to provide a home for her and the baby. I thought she'd be happy...."

Drake trailed off, puzzled and irritated with Maya's

stubborn insistence that he find his soul before coming to her with his heart.

"Women like to be consulted on these things," his father said, obviously trying to be kind. "Talk to her some more. If you really want to settle down to an office job, Colton Enterprises has plenty of positions that can use a good mover and shaker."

"Thanks." Drake managed to smile at his dad. "Things certainly aren't going as I expected. I arrived home on the sixth, fully expecting to be a married man by the seventh. Here it is, twelve days later. I'm a father, but no closer to being a husband that I can tell."

"Is it a question of caring?"

I love you.

Drake shook his head. "She...cares. So do I. It's more a question of seeing eye to eye about the future."

"Talk to her. Don't let happiness slip through your fingers without fighting to hold on to it with all your might."

"I don't intend to," Drake assured the other man, feeling heartened by the conversation. He and Maya shared a child and a wild, sweet passion. She'd said she loved him. How could he make her see they belonged together?

"The rain is starting," Joe said. "We'd better go in. I have a conference call with Peter and Emmett in a bit. Emmett wants to expand our oil operations. Peter says it isn't a good time because of overproduction among the OPEC countries."

"Speaking for myself, I'd listen to Peter."

"He's a good man," his father agreed as they headed for the sunroom door.

The men went to the den for a brandy. Drake lit a fire and settled in an easy chair as the mist turned to a downpour.

Louise Smith woke with tears pouring down her cheeks. Outside, the Mississippi night had turned stormy, just as it had the other night when she'd woken from a nightmare. This time, it wasn't a little red-haired girl she'd seen in her dreams, but two baby boys, as alike as two peas.

Twins.

Somehow she knew they were hers. She'd had at least one child, the doctors had told her.

Where, oh, where were those babies?

She rocked back and forth, her heart locked in turmoil and pain. She couldn't bear it. She had to know. She had to find the past and face whatever horror it held, no matter how much it hurt.

Those babies…they needed her. Her sweet lost babies…oh, God, the babies…

"Please, please," she whispered. "My children…my husband—"

She pressed a hand over her mouth as the dark man appeared in her vision, his expression that of one stricken with unhappiness. He was real. So were the babies.

She'd been married. She had children. Once she had loved and been loved.

"I know it! I know it!" she cried. "Where are you?"

Only the howling wind answered. A torrent of raindrops hit the windows as if the world cried with her, echoing her grief.

"Please, God, please help me find them," she prayed, fearing she was coming to the end of her tether, that the insanity that had once claimed her would do so again.

Lost in the darkness of her mind, she might never find her past...or the love she'd once known.

Her husband. Her babies. The red-haired girl who was now a woman. Other faces of other people, some children, some adults. She needed them. And they needed her. She was certain of it. They were in danger, grave danger. She felt it to the depths of her soul. And only she could save them.

"Oh, please...please," she cried. "Heavenly Father, help me. Help *them*."

Lightning flashed with a tremendous brightness and thunder rolled over the land with a great roar that shook buildings and rattled windows.

"Joe," she screamed, but the fury of the storm drowned out the word. It was terrifying, but no worse than the storm within.

Eleven

On Monday, six days after Marissa's birth, Maya resumed her full duties. After getting Joe and Teddy off to school, she read a chapter in a book on early childhood, then napped until lunch. After eating, she gathered Marissa, then headed for the Hopechest Ranch.

Drake was waiting out front for her. "Ride with me," he requested. "I told my father I'd look over the children's ranch with an eye toward something we can do to improve it."

"You should talk to your sister. Amber knows more than anyone about the financial conditions and needs of the children."

"Good idea," he said equably, helping her and Marissa into his truck. "You have any suggestions?"

Before she quite knew how it happened, she was

riding along with Drake, discussing the children's needs at the Hopechest, which served as a foster home, juvenile retention center and school for kids with various hardships in their young lives.

"Supplies," Maya said as he parked near the classroom where she tutored her students. "Books, especially. That's the main thing I think we need. The kids need books that show other kids overcoming sad lives and becoming successful citizens. Also art supplies—chalk and sketch paper. Oh, and workbooks in math would be good, too. Maybe we could get some of those self-tutoring computer programs?"

"Sure."

Maya realized she was waxing on and on when Drake gave her an amused smile. She shut up and went into her assigned room. There, she directed Drake to deposit the baby carrier holding the sleeping Marissa beside the desk.

"I'll look up the Hopechest director," he said, "and talk to him. I'll pick you up at three to head back to our place. Okay?"

She nodded, carefully not looking at him as she set out her folders and papers. Johnny met Drake at the door. The two males spoke in passing of the coming weekend and the plans for roping. Sighing, she admitted Drake was so good for Johnny and his younger brothers. He was someone they could look up to and emulate.

Well, to a point. She didn't want the boys to dwell on past misfortunes as Drake seemed to do. Most particularly, Johnny needed to move beyond his troublesome past to a secure future.

"How did you do with the problems Mr. Martin gave you?" she asked, pulling a new novel for him out of her briefcase.

"Fine. I think."

He gave her a self-satisfied grin, which told her he'd thought the assignment was an easy one. "Don't get cheeky," she told him affectionately, taking the homework paper.

"Is this your baby?" he asked, bending over the sleeping baby.

"Yes. Meet Marissa Joy…Colton." She paused, then plunged on, knowing the news wasn't a secret. "Drake is her father."

"Are you going to get married?"

Maya studied the teenager carefully, sure there were other questions behind this one, but not sure she wanted to answer them. "We're discussing it," she at last said, which was an honest answer. "It's difficult to know what to do. His job in the SEALs takes him all over the world, to places a wife and baby can't go."

"So, couldn't you stay here and he could come home between assignments? I had a friend whose dad was in the Navy. He was away for months at a time. I think they were mostly glad. He beat up on them when he came home."

Maya just shook her head at the matter-of-fact manner this news was delivered. How did children ever grow up to be decent, caring people in this crazy world? Johnny, for instance, was kind and enthusiastic and intelligent. How had his finer qualities ever survived his early years?

"Some people need to take a course or two in anger management," she said dryly.

Johnny looked surprised. "There must be courses in everything. I'm going to get a college degree. I can work my way through, just like you, only maybe as a cowhand instead of a baby-sitter."

Her heart warmed as he cast her an admiring glance, then quickly looked away. These were the moments a teacher lived for—seeing the results of your efforts pay off in a student's desire to learn more.

Teaching was definitely the career for her, so she'd done one thing right. It was the rest of her life that was in turmoil. She swallowed as yearning overcame reasoning. She wanted to follow her heart and forget the problems that, at midnight, seemed insurmountable.

"Let's get to work," she said huskily. "I brought you a new book. The kids in this story have an interesting adventure. I liked the way their characters developed as the story progressed."

For the next two hours she concentrated on her tasks, putting aside her own worries as she taught her students how to decipher letters to make sounds, then words, then sentences that made sense. She was pleasantly surprised to see that Johnny had indeed handled the problems just fine.

"Next time they'll be harder," she promised, giving him a narrow-eyed scrutiny that made him laugh.

"She's really tough," Drake said, entering the room.

"Yeah." With another laugh, the teenager picked

up the new adventure novel about three kids who got lost from their family and managed to find their way home, learning and growing as they worked together to make it.

Before the trip back to the hacienda, Marissa awoke and demanded her lunch.

"When does she eat?" Drake asked.

"When she wants to. I'm following a feed-on-demand philosophy at present. When she's a month old, I'll gradually work into scheduled feedings. At least, that's my plan. Putting it into action may be something different."

His chuckle warmed her heart. Lifting the baby, she unbuttoned her blouse and lowered the nursing bra. Marissa suckled in her usual noisy way, then fell into a light slumber. Maya tapped her on the cheek to remind her to stick with the business at hand.

The baby roused with an irritated cry, then nursed again. Each time she fell asleep, Maya woke her.

"Maybe she's not hungry," Drake suggested.

"If she demands a meal, then she has to cooperate. I don't want her to develop the habit of eating just enough to take the edge off her appetite, then falling asleep. I can't nurse her every few minutes."

"I see."

"I'm lucky that I can have her with me while I work. It must be terribly hard on those parents who can't."

Drake nodded thoughtfully. "I'd like for you to show me how to take care of her, if you don't mind. I figure I'd better start now in preparation for those times when she stays with me and I have to do everything.''

Stunned by the implications of this statement, Maya could only stare at him for a few seconds. She finally asked, ''Are you planning on her living with you?''

''It's traditional for fathers to get their kids during vacations and holidays, isn't it?''

Maya could scarcely breathe, much less answer. ''I—I suppose. Would you want to do that? A child is a lot of responsibility. You couldn't go off—''

''I know that,'' he said when she stopped, her thoughts in a muddle.

Maya finished the feeding session and they made their way silently back to the house. Drake carried the infant seat, diaper bag and her briefcase inside.

''Drake,'' Teddy called, coming from the family theater over the five-car garage and clambering down the steps. ''Can we do some roping now?''

''You have homework first,'' Maya reminded them.

''Why do we always have to do dumb homework?'' Joe Junior groused, following his brother.

''Because you did poorly on your math,'' Drake answered. ''Maya's going to teach me to bathe Marissa. You two get your work done, then we'll talk about roping.''

Joe wrinkled his nose in disbelief. ''You're going to give Marissa a bath? She's just a baby.''

''Yeah, and a girl,'' Teddy added, as if this were the crowning insult.

''I happen to like girls,'' Drake told the younger

boys with a grin. "Especially when they're as pretty as their mama."

His look of frank admiration produced the familiar longing. Flustered, she led the way to her room.

"Can we watch?" Teddy wanted to know, obviously curious about this aspect of adulthood. "Is it hard to give babies baths? Hey, maybe we can help."

"You can powder her," Maya promised.

She showed them the little plastic washbasin she used for the baby. "Stick your elbow in to test the temperature."

Each male solemnly bared his elbow and checked the water. "Feels okay to me," Joe said, going first.

The other two agreed it did.

She showed them how to undress Marissa, holding her head so it didn't bobble and stripping the gown and diaper off. "Put your left arm under her head and hold on to her left arm. That way she can't wriggle free when she's all slippery with soap."

She showed them how.

"Okay, we can take over now, can't we, men?" Drake asked.

"Sure," the boys said, full of confidence.

Maya, not at all sure this was the thing to do, sat in the rocking chair and watched the operation through the open door to the bathroom. With much discussion and some adult chuckling and little-boy giggling, they washed the baby, then powdered and dressed her.

Drake, she saw, was quite competent at the task. During the past six days, he'd watched everything she did, staying close to her and the baby during most of their waking hours. It was almost like being married.

Almost, but not quite.

Her heart clenched as she thought of the days and years ahead. If Drake was planning on making a place in his life for his daughter, that was good, wasn't it? Didn't it show he was willing to accommodate a family? Maybe she was being stubborn, as he said.

Sitting at her desk, she checked her e-mail and phone messages, then the boys' papers from their day at school. By the time she finished, the guys were finished, too. The baby, with a wise stare at Maya, closed her eyes and went right to sleep when placed in her bassinet.

"She's a good baby, isn't she?" Drake said, watching his sleeping daughter.

"Yes."

"Maya, was I a good baby?" Teddy demanded.

Maya grinned. "You cried all night, every night, for the first month."

He laughed. "What about Joe?"

"He knew he'd found a good home from the first. He hardly ever cried. But when he did, look out! He could keep it up for hours." She smiled, then gestured toward the other end of the room. "Now, homework."

The boys took their places at each side of her desk and dutifully opened their books. Drake settled in the rocking chair with a magazine on parenting. Maya continued reading her book on childhood development. That was how Ms. Meredith found them when she came in.

"Well, if this isn't the cozy family scene," she said, pausing in the open doorway.

Maya stiffened at the sarcastic undertone, but she managed a calm smile. It didn't do to let the other woman see that she could upset her.

"Hello, darlings," Meredith went on. "Don't you have a kiss for your mother?"

The boys leaped up from their homework and rushed to Meredith's arms, where they were soundly kissed and petted. Their mother gave them each a bag of candy and permission to eat it. Maya refrained from mentioning dinner was less than two hours away.

Meredith questioned the boys extensively about their activities, lavishing attention on them as she hadn't done in days. Or weeks, Maya thought. In fact, Ms. Meredith had seemed distracted, her temper more uncertain, since…since Joe's birthday party.

Well, it must be pretty scary when someone took a shot at your husband. Anyone would be distracted.

However, Joe had been a U.S. Senator in the past. He'd struck it rich in oil long ago, then moved into other enterprises. A man in his position would make enemies no matter how nice he really was. People were jealous—

Another thought occurred to Maya. Ms. Meredith acted almost jealous of her own husband, not because of other women, but because their children obviously loved and respected their father. It struck Maya as very odd.

Recalling the conversation with Drake about his

mother being different, she felt a chill creep along her scalp. What was going on in the Colton household?

At nine-thirty, Maya entered the living room where Drake, holding Marissa, talked with his father. He'd taken over the care of the baby while she supervised the boys' baths and saw them to bed. The scene between father and son looked so peaceful, she hated to intrude.

"Excuse me. I thought I'd get Marissa now and put her to bed." She hovered at the hall doorway.

"Come in, Maya," Joe invited. "Won't you join us for a few minutes? Men need the company of women to keep us up on our manners, don't we, son?"

"Uh, right. Anything you say, Dad," Drake agreed with wry humor.

He gave her a once-over that brought a glow to her face. She'd showered and put on a long skirt and top outfit in dramatic red and black that complemented her coloring, one she hadn't been able to wear for five months. Tonight she felt attractive as a woman again.

Choosing an easy chair, she sighed as she relaxed, the many demands of the day at last over.

"Tired?" Joe asked kindly.

She hesitated about admitting a weakness, then nodded. "The longest the baby has slept at a time has been three hours. I didn't realize waking several times during the night would be so draining."

During the past week, she'd often wondered how her mother had made it, caring for this big house, planning and cooking meals, then keeping her own home clean and neat as well as taking care of a husband and two children. All her memories were of a happy, tireless woman who rarely got cranky or complained about all the work to be done. Maya didn't think she was made of the same caliber stuff.

Then, having admitted fatigue, she worried that Joe would think she was neglecting her duties to his sons. "Joe and Teddy have been wonderful about helping with the baby. And getting their homework done without coaxing."

"Good. If they give you any trouble, let me know." The older man stared out at the dark patio, his expression frowning and thoughtful.

"Maya needs weekends off," Drake said suddenly. "She works seven days a week. I'm pretty sure that's against the labor laws."

His father swung his head around, his eyes narrowed as he studied his son. Drake gave him a level stare.

"You're right, son. Maya, my apologies to you. I've been so caught up in…other things, I've not paid much attention to the younger boys or the number of hours you've been putting in."

"It's okay," she hastened to assure him. "Mom helps when I need it. That is, when she's not busy in the house or with meals. And Dad, too, when he's not working on the garden."

She realized her whole family was beholden to the Coltons for their livelihood. By choice, though. Both her parents had been offered high salaries and other benefits by visitors to the hacienda who had seen their work.

"A family that plays together, stays together," Joe murmured. "Working together is important, too, or just being there for each other."

Drake cast a quiet glance her way, his gaze filled with dark thoughts that she sensed were painful.

"You were there," she reminded him, "when Marissa was born. You helped…" She lost the thought as his perusal sharpened.

"But I wasn't with you during the months before that."

She sensed the criticism he directed at himself. He wasn't a man who could easily brush off his failings. "You didn't know. I'm sorry for not writing. I realize I should have. You had a right to know about the baby."

His eyes locked with hers as golden threads of longing arced between them, reminding her of all the things she loved about this man. That he was honorable went without saying. That he was gentle and caring and considerate was also true. He took his responsibilities seriously.

Perhaps she was being stubborn and proud, thinking only of her own bruised feelings after reading that note.

There's no place in my life for a wife and family.

Those words still caused an ache inside, indicating as they did that he'd only had a brief time for her as a lover, but nothing more. She shook her head slightly, denying the pain. Regret was a useless emotion unless it brought a change in future actions.

If she had been positive he loved her, she would have accepted his proposal and tried to help him with the past. However, she wouldn't become an added responsibility, their lovemaking yet another mistake he had to atone for.

That was the unkindest cut of all, she mused, borrowing a phrase from Shakespeare. That he considered their time together a mistake, one that he would have to pay for in marriage and child support all his life, brought such a flurry of regret on her part that she wanted to put her head down and cry out her misery.

Of course she didn't. Instead, she smiled and listened to the men chat about the various Colton projects and children, both natural and foster.

Marissa woke, stretched, then nuzzled Drake's shirt. Not finding what she wanted, she screwed up her face and let out a wail.

"Here, Mom, I think this is your department," Drake said with a smile. He brought the baby to her.

She rose, intending to go to her room, but Joe gestured for her to be seated.

"There's something special about a mother nursing her child," he said. "It brings out the most tender of feelings in men."

"Yes," Drake agreed. "And protective, too. Having a child puts things in a different perspective."

Maya saw the two men exchange a look as she settled down to feed the hungry baby, who stopped crying as soon as she found the nourishment she wanted. When it was time to burp the child, Drake took Marissa from her, laid the baby across his knees and patted her back.

"She likes this position best," he told his dad, sounding very much an expert on the subject.

"Michael preferred that one, too, but you always had to be up on my shoulder where you could see what was going on. You used to scrutinize everyone who came into the room. If you didn't like their looks, you bellowed until they left."

Maya laughed at this picture of the young Drake.

"You hear that?" Drake asked the baby in jest. "She's laughing at your ol' dad, kid." He got up and brought Marissa back to Maya. As he laid her in Maya's arms, the back of his finger brushed lightly against her breast. Flames shot to the spot, then swept outward to every point in her body. He must have felt it, too.

Immediately he moved away. "Sorry," he murmured.

She nodded self-consciously, hating the blush she could feel invading her face.

Joe stood up. "You young people will have to excuse me. It's been a long day, and I think I'll go along to my room. There's a report I need to look over before I go to bed."

Maya echoed Drake's "Good night" as the older man left them. She wondered if Joe thought they should be alone.

To work out their problems?

He was kind and thoughtful, but she didn't want to be alone with Drake. It was too dangerous to her peace of mind. She shifted the baby to the other breast to finish feeding.

"I wish I had the right to touch you without apology," Drake said, taking her by surprise.

"Wh-what do you mean?"

"If we were married, would I have to apologize for accidentally brushing against you?"

She didn't answer as she helped the baby latch on. Wincing as her breasts gave that funny, almost painful, sensation—her milk coming down, her mother had told her—she slowly shook her head.

He snorted ruefully. "You had to think about it long enough before answering."

"I wasn't sure what to say. Even if we were married, I'm not sure what rights we would have...over each other," she added.

"All the rights of a husband and wife to caress and touch each other and to enjoy each other's company."

"Physically?"

He became thoughtful. "That's part of it, but not all. There're other ways of sharing. Like now. I like watching you while our daughter nurses. It makes me remember touching you there and how much I enjoyed it. I know we can't make love until the doctor checks you out, but I like thinking about it and how you responded. Those little breathy cries drove me wild."

Aghast at his candid remarks, she gave him a repressive scowl. "I'm not going to continue an affair with you, Drake," she informed him stoically, meaning it, yet afraid she wouldn't be able to hold to that decision if he pursued her.

"I thought that was part of marriage."

He gave her his most innocent look, which was totally belied by the sexy simmer in his eyes.

"Oh. Marriage."

"Yes, marriage." He took a deep breath. "I'll not settle for less between us. Our daughter deserves a settled family life. As well as our other children."

Maya gasped. "Are you suggesting... Do you think that I, that we..."

"Yes, we will."

She could only stare at him in shock.

"It will happen. We're too volatile together. There's need and hunger and feelings between us. We've shared too much. I've told you about the ghosts that haunt me from the past. Is it fair to use that to keep me at a distance?"

Maya lowered her head, not sure what to say.

"Is it?" he persisted softly. "I've offered you a future with me as my wife. I want to help raise our child." He paused, then went on quietly, "I want other children. With you. You're the only woman I can see as their mother."

"That's not fair, Drake."

"It's true. You are my future. If you're not it, then I don't know what it will be. I'm tired of the dark, Maya. Give me the sunshine of your love, and I'll pledge you my future, my love, anything you want. If you'll but have me."

The hot, desperate tears clawed at her throat. "A humble Drake?" she managed to say with only a slight tremor in her voice. "Is this the man we know and love?"

He slid a finger under her chin and gently lifted so that their eyes met. "I hope so," he said sincerely. "We have a beautiful daughter. We've shared a great passion. Surely that's enough for a beginning."

"Maybe."

"Then, marriage?"

She shook her head. "I can't. There's something, a barrier...I can't explain."

He sighed. "Okay. I have to finish my present assignment. That will give us six months to discuss and plan for the future. I'll call, and we can e-mail each other. Will you give me that time?"

Staring into his eyes, she nodded, not sure what she was promising.

"In the meantime, I want to be part of your life for the rest of my leave. Let's relax and enjoy our baby."

His mood changed, his grin becoming cocky and entirely too knowing when it came to her, but love, she found, was stronger than pride or fear or any other emotion. She had to take a chance and see where this might lead.

"All right," she said.

He clutched his heart. "The lady agrees. I must be dreaming."

She joined in his laughter, hearing a new note in it. No, not new, old—the old Drake of long ago.

Perhaps there was a future for them after all.

Twelve

"**W**here are you?" Patsy Portman, who had called herself Meredith Colton for ten years, demanded. "It's about time you called."

"I'm in Redding. I've got some news," Silas Pike, who preferred to be called "Snake Eyes," told her. "You want to hear it or not?"

"Of course I want to hear it! Have you found Emily?"

"Not exactly—"

Patsy huffed in exasperation. "I'm not sending you any more money."

"Will you hold on to your horses and let me finish?" he demanded belligerently. "I found the trucker who picked her up, some hayseed driving a hay truck."

He laughed as if he'd said something extraordinarily witty. Patsy rolled her eyes. "And?"

"He gave her a ride to Wyoming."

"Big deal. We already suspected she was in Wyoming."

Obviously considering himself a super-sleuth, Silas gave his little self-satisfied laugh. "Now we have proof. Some regulars in this truck stop recall her asking about some hick town of Needle Creek."

Patsy could feel her flesh tingle. "*Nettle* Creek?" She'd nearly forgotten about the McGrath homestead where Joe had been raised. She hadn't been there and had no desire to go to that godforsaken place in the middle of nowhere. Prosperino was bad enough, thank you very much! "You fool, Pike. It's Nettle Creek. She must have gone to her uncle Peter's place."

"I know all about him. As I see it, all I have to do is mosey on up to Nettle Creek, find the McGrath place, and bingo, we'll have the kid."

"Well, do it," Patsy instructed. "And hurry. Things aren't looking good on this end."

They made arrangements to talk in three days' time and hung up. Patsy slipped the tiny cell phone into her pocket. It produced a pulse she could feel against her thigh instead of ringing, so no one knew when she got a call. Joe didn't even know about the phone. She'd gotten it under a fictitious name.

Smiling with delight at fooling Joe and his watchdogs—that hateful Peter McGrath and his daughter Heather, now married to that nosy detective, Thaddeus Law, and Joe's stupid kids—she danced around the room. When her elated mood passed, she went over the situation again.

Letting Emily Blair Colton live after the accident ten years ago had been a mistake. She should have bashed in the brat's head after she'd forced Meredith off the road and into the ditch.

But she'd had to get rid of Meredith at the time. Unable to take the chance that a body might be found and discovered to be the real Meredith, she'd hit on another, quite brilliant plan.

Meredith hadn't known what was happening when Patsy delivered her to the clinic for the criminally insane where she'd once been held. That had worked out great.

In fact, other than the glitch of getting pregnant with Teddy, life had worked out according to plan. Everything had been going fine until Joe's birthday party.

Whoever had shot at him had ruined *her* plans. Joe'd been all ready to drink his glass of champagne—which contained a nasty little birthday present from her personally—when that idiot had fired...and missed! Joe had dropped the glass without touching a drop.

It was discouraging. With Emily's increasingly frequent nightmares about the accident and insisting there had been two Merediths at the scene, one good and one evil, Patsy had no choice but to get rid of the girl, who was now a young woman. That was why she'd had to hire Snake Eyes.

All this extra worry left her with no time to concentrate on getting rid of Joe and finding her sweet baby, Jewel, and looking for a house of her own. Maybe in San Francisco. One of those mansions down at the marina perhaps, or in Pacific Heights. Lombard Street, the block billed as the crookedest street in the world, was elite, but there were all those tourists to deal with. Nob Hill, of course, was quite passé.

She sighed as she settled on the silk brocade lounge chair. Her life was too complicated by far. She liked the current notion of simplifying things. Which was exactly what she was trying to do. With Joe and Emily—and Snake Eyes Pike—out of the way, her life would be much simpler. She laughed and laughed at the idea.

Emily Blair Colton studied herself in the mirror. A natural chestnut redhead, she wondered if she should dye her hair to make it harder for anyone to trace her. The kind trucker who had given her the ride to Wyoming might easily recall a redhead, but could he identify her if she were a blonde or brunette?

Turning, she paced the room.

Was she being paranoid about her adoptive mother and the evil twin? Perhaps the creep who had tried to murder her had no connection to her nightmares concerning the accident years ago and her dreams, or memories, of seeing two Merediths, one dazed and shaken from the auto wreck, holding her head where she bled from a cut, and the other Meredith, a gleeful smile on her face, coaxing the injured Meredith into the unknown vehicle that had swerved at them and forced their car off the road.

Emily had passed out then from her own injuries. When she'd come to, safe in the hospital, there had only been one Meredith. Everyone had assured her she was suffering hallucinations, but there was one thing—her mother had never called her "Sparrow" again after that. She didn't seem to recall the nickname she'd given Emily.

There'd been other changes, too, little things too numerous to overlook, but not obvious enough to warrant an investigation. Anyhow, how did you investigate a *feeling* that things weren't right?

Her best friend and cousin, Liza Colton, had believed her from the first. Now Rand, the oldest Colton son, seemed nearly convinced, too. He'd asked Austin McGrath check out their mother. Mother? Emily thought of her as the evil twin from her nightmares.

Pain pierced her heart. What had happened to the good Meredith, the tender woman who had adopted her and saved her from a life of loneliness and fear when she was orphaned?

Whatever the cost, she knew they had to find out the truth. She needed to call Rand and see if Austin had learned anything more about Meredith's past. She'd always been rather silent about her youth.

Emily put on her new heavy coat and started off for work. Her job as a waitress gave her the means to stay in Keyhole, where she felt safe. Sort of.

Rand thought she should come stay with him, but she was afraid she'd be traced too easily to her oldest brother. He agreed everything was in a mess concerning her disappearance and she was still in grave danger.

Someone had collected the ransom money Joe had paid for her safe return, but who?

The supposed kidnapper was pretty bold to demand ransom when he didn't even have a victim. Was he or she a mere opportunist? Or was the evil Meredith in cahoots with someone else?

Tears burned as Emily trudged to the café, entered the back door and hung up her warm clothing. There seemed no end to the nightmare her life had become.

Toby Atkins was at the café counter when she started on duty. "Hi," he said, putting his coffee cup down.

The young law officer was blond and handsome in a boyish way, although Emily had to admit his lanky, six-foot frame wasn't boyish in the least. He contributed to her feeling of safety in the small town, but his attention was troublesome, too. He was both suspicious of her and interested in a man-woman way.

There was certainly no room in her life at present to even consider that kind of thing. She was doing her best just to stay alive!

Drake entered the kitchen where Maya and her mom worked quietly together in the manner of women who had long done so. He found it comforting in a way his own family life had rarely been. There was a graciousness in the Ramirez family dealings with each other, their caring for each other always forming the backdrop of their relationship.

The dark cloud of past mistakes seemed to draw closer as he thought of the Coltons. An ominous sense of foreboding gathered inside him. He wasn't sure if it was due to his past or to the present worries. He'd talked to Rand last night, but neither had any new information.

Today was Wednesday, the first day of March. He'd arrived on the sixth. Almost a month.

Whenever he came upon Maya, an incredible burst of anticipation overrode common sense. He wanted to go to her, to kiss her until they were both breathless.

Although he knew better than to expect total happiness, being with her and the baby brought a new dimension to his days. True, life had a way of slapping a person down and reminding one of the grim realities, yet he was aware of a lightness to his step whenever he headed for the house, knowing his two girls were there.

His?

The scar on his hip throbbed, as if his body wanted to caution him about expecting too much of the future.

"I'm going to my room to change," he told the two women. "I'll see you at lunch."

"Right." Maya watched him go, her heart righting itself with an effort. It was scary to love someone so much and know your happiness was in his hands.

"It will work out," her mother said unexpectedly.

"Will it?" She didn't see how. Hearing Marissa whimper through the baby monitor, she hurried to her room.

The baby cried during the diaper change, but stopped when Maya sat in the rocker and played hand-clapping games and talked nonsense with her.

After stimulating Marissa into wakefulness, she nursed the baby, her thoughts in limbo as she stared out at the rolling land and hills surrounding the ranch.

Outside, it was a cold, clear winter day. Friday was supposed to be misty, according to the weather report that morning. A chill attacked her heart, and she wished for the warmth of summer. She'd always assumed she would be a June bride. She smiled at the mockery of it all. Here she was a mother without ever being a bride.

After nursing Marissa, she put the baby in the bassinet. Her father had gotten her old crib from the attic of their house and was in the middle of repainting it. He'd promised it would be ready by the end of the week.

She liked the idea of having the bed for her baby. Then she wondered where she and Drake and Marissa would be by the end of March. So much seemed to have happened already—his return, the birth, now a new element had entered their relationship. He stayed close to them, holding the baby and rocking her, helping with bathtime. There was that new undernote of happiness in him, too.

It almost made the darkness disappear. Almost.

"Mom, the monitor is on," she said through the intercom. "I'm going to go over Joe's math homework with Ms. Meredith. Yell if you hear the baby."

Her mother answered through the central unit. Maya picked up the school papers from her desk and headed for her boss's quarters. She really dreaded facing the woman, as her mood swings were completely unpredictable.

Just as she started down the hall of the south wing, she saw Drake slip into his mother's room.

Maya slowed, wondering if she should interrupt. However, Ms. Meredith had given orders for a daily report on Joe's progress with percent problems. Maya walked on. At the closed door, she hesitated again, then knocked.

No answer.

The hair prickled on the back of her neck. She knocked again. Still no answer. All was silent.

Drake's being in his mother's room when she apparently wasn't there struck Maya as odd. She quietly opened the door. "What are you doing?" she asked.

Drake was bending over an open drawer of Meredith's desk. He jerked around with a glare, then smiled.

"Caught in the act. I must be getting careless," he said, then shrugged. "I'm obviously going through my mother's things."

"Why?"

"I'm out of pocket money and thought I'd steal some?" he suggested.

"Huh."

"You won't go for that?"

"No. What are you looking for? Where is your mother?"

"She decided to go to San Francisco for the day. I'm looking for clues."

Maya laid Joe's math homework, graded and returned by his teacher, on Ms. Meredith's desk. "To what?"

"Anything. I don't really know," he added at her frown.

"Does this have to do with the questions you asked me before, the ones about your mother?"

"Give me a minute, then we'll talk."

Maya shut up and watched him thoroughly go through the desk, including checking every drawer and the desk itself for hidden compartments, she supposed. He looked through a file drawer, whistled when he saw the duns and the amount of money she owed to various merchants, then moved on. He then proceeded to search the rest of the room just as thoroughly.

"Nothing," he said at last. "Let's go."

Taking her arm, he ushered her into his room. Maya wasn't at all sure about being alone with him in his bedroom. It was a familiar place and brought back remembered ecstasy. And remembered pain.

He closed the door and leaned against it. "Trapped," he murmured without a smile to show he was teasing.

The latent fire in his eyes warmed her clear through. "What were you looking for?" she asked.

"Evidence that my mother isn't the woman she claims to be."

Maya recalled their previous conversations about the changes in his mother, about the fact that she'd had a twin. But he'd told her the twin had died. The implications became clear. She clutched a hand to her chest. "Surely you don't think... You can't possibly believe..."

"What?"

"That this twin… No, it's too preposterous!"

"Is it?" He paced the room. "Things have changed, but when did it happen? Mother was different after the accident that time when she was taking Emily to visit her biological grandmother."

"When Emily thought she saw two Merediths."

"Yes."

Maya had never seen Drake look so grim. "Have you talked to Sophie or Amber about this?"

"No, only Rand. As you said, it's too preposterous."

"But it could be true."

"Then you believe me?"

"Of course," she said, giving it no further thought.

He stopped in front of her. "Thank you. Sometimes it seems as if we must be crazy, that no one could carry on a charade for ten years."

"Unless you were an identical twin." She considered her studies of personality types. "Con artists are very good at insinuating themselves into people's lives. They're like chameleons. They take on the protective coloring of their surroundings. How can I help?"

A muscle moved in his jaw. "Just by being here," he murmured, his eyes boring into hers.

She didn't move when he slipped his hands behind her neck and, using his thumbs, held her face up to his. She knew his intention, but she stayed still.

The kiss was gentle and sweet, so sweet. It flowed into her like warm syrup, soothing a place in her soul. She breathed deeply of him, drawing his scent into her lungs, filling herself with him, this man.

Drake. Beloved.

Lifting her arms, she held on to his shoulders, feeling the strength he kept in check as he pulled her closer. For some reason, she was reminded of their first kiss last summer, the tenderness of it, the questioning of the emotion behind the kiss, the hunger that went deeper than the mere physical.

"I need you," he whispered, pressing her cheek to his chest and planting kisses along her temple. "It's always there, an ache that won't go away."

She could have wept at the despair in his voice. "I don't want to hurt you. I want you to be happy," she told him, clutching his shirt.

He cupped her face again and nibbled at her lips in little hungry forays that didn't near satisfy her need for the taste and feel of him. "You are my happiness."

She shook her head, knowing the darkness still possessed his soul, sensing it even as he touched and caressed her. She held him tightly, as if to give him her warmth, as if her love might brighten that dark area.

"Maya," he said, his voice hoarse with intensity. "My sweet lover, my dream come true. Let me hold you, just for a while. I've missed you."

The hunger swept up from that deep well of need that only he stirred. "This is no good," she tried to tell him, even as she caressed and stroked. "We have to think—"

He lifted his head, his eyes haunted. "Perhaps that's been our problem. We think too much, you and

I. I need to touch you, to remember how you feel in my arms.''

"Why? We can't go any further."

"Shh," he said. "I just want to hold you, that's all. It's enough for now."

Shaking her head helplessly, she let him enfold her and felt the bitterness of the past few months fade from memory. She lifted her face to his, the sweetness of the moment filling her whole being.

He kissed her deeply, with passion held carefully in check, his hands roaming her back, his strong fingers massaging her flesh as if finding the reality of her through his touch.

Sensing his longing, she returned the kiss, satisfying her own yearning for him.

"I miss those little cries you used to make," he told her, nipping at her lips, her ear, her throat. "I wake at night, thinking I can hear you, and realize it's only a dream. Lying in a tent in the jungle, I think of you. On maneuvers in the desert. Parachuting onto an ice floe. It doesn't matter. You go wherever I go."

"But only in your dreams," she reminded him, feeling the hurt of his leaving all over again, even as she returned his kisses. "It's never real."

"It was real last summer. We created a child."

Pressing her forehead against his chest, she swallowed painfully. "We were both foolish. We shouldn't be again."

He opened a button and trailed kisses downward. Another button. More kisses. She closed her eyes and tried to concentrate on breathing.

"I've told myself the same thing. But holding you doesn't feel foolish. It's good, so good."

The husky passion thrilled her now as it had in June. When he sat on the bed, she went with him willingly, settling in his lap as the hot passion built between them.

"So strong," she whispered. "I never knew this could be so strong, the need so compelling."

"I know. It's the same with me. Nothing, no one else, can begin to satisfy it."

"Yes," she said on a gasp when he finished unfastening the buttons and pushed the blouse off her shoulders.

"I need to feel you against me, skin on skin." His eyes were molten, his expression one of intense wonder.

Hands trembling, she helped him slip out of his long-sleeved shirt, an old flannel one he'd had for ages. He eased them gently down on his bed, until they were lying side by side, his arm under her head.

"We lay like this the first time, remember? I was inside you, and we stayed together like this."

"Yes, I remember," she said softly, lost in the past and all the wonderful misty dreams she harbored about them. "Being together...so new and wonderful."

"And magic. All that magic."

"I didn't know you felt it."

"Every time I looked at you, touched you, it was the same. You glowed from inside, like some kind of fire I couldn't ignore."

"It was the same for me," she told him, spellbound all over again.

He took a deep breath, let it out slowly. Propping himself on an elbow, he drew smaller and smaller circles on her breasts, first one, then the other. Two tiny damp spots appeared on the satiny material of her bra.

Slowly, carefully, he peeled one nursing flap open. A drop of milk appeared on her nipple. He bent and touched his tongue to it. "The stuff of life," he whispered. "It's in you, part of you, of the magic. No wonder we made a child."

She stroked the hair from his forehead. "It's part of you, too, Drake. The spark came from both of us, not me alone. It took both of us."

"I know. I still can't believe it."

"I can. You have so much goodness inside you. I've always known it."

"How?" he asked, pain in his eyes. He shook his head as if he didn't understand. "How can you see goodness when I see only darkness?"

She had no answer. Pulling his head down, she held him close, needing to comfort his lost, questing heart.

Bending, he kissed her exposed breast tenderly, then laved up the drops of nourishment. Closing the bra, he kissed along her neck while he held and explored her with the greatest tenderness she had ever known.

"You're the one good thing," he told her, "the only good thing in my life, you and the baby."

She wanted to ask why he wouldn't let them be part of his life, but she didn't. This moment was special, and they'd had few of those during the past month.

"Hold me," she whispered.

"I will," he said and it sounded like a promise.

The moments flew past. Thirty minutes. An hour. And still he held and caressed her, taking them no farther than deep kisses and playful explorations of her mouth with his.

He cupped his body around hers, laying her legs over his thighs as he'd done the last time they'd made love. Still propped on one arm, he touched her over and over—breasts, waist, thighs—as if he couldn't get enough of the wonder of her.

"You make my heart sing," she said at one point. She lightly ran her fingertips through the wiry patch of hair on his chest.

He smiled, his gaze peaceful, as if these stolen moments together had soothed something in his soul, although there was still tense passion in his body.

"We need to marry," he said.

"Not yet."

"When?"

"I don't know."

"We can work it out."

His words conveyed confidence, but she shook her head. "You're not ready."

"Promise me something." He traced the outline of her lips, making her mouth burn for more of his kisses.

"What?"

"That in six months, whether you think I'm ready or not, you'll accept my proposal."

She tried to ignore the clamor of her too-eager heart. "If you ask again at that time, then I'll accept."

"Shall we tell our parents we're engaged?"

She wasn't that sure of the future. "I'd rather not."

For a moment, he didn't say anything, then he nodded and rose. Holding out a hand, he helped her up. They fastened their clothing and left his room.

"I still want to help with the mystery about your mother," she told him. "If there is a mystery."

"Something will break soon. I have a gut feeling about it. Austin or Thaddeus or someone will find a clue we've overlooked. Then we'll know."

A shiver went down her spine as they walked to her room to check on Marissa. Her mother was there, rocking the baby and singing quietly in Spanish.

Inez smiled benevolently at them as she stood. "She's been an angel. I just wanted to hold her."

"Thanks," Drake said. He took the baby and settled in the rocker. "Rocking a baby is relaxing, isn't it?"

Inez looked from him to his daughter, then laughed softly. "Yes, indeed." Still smiling, she left them.

Maya caught a glimpse of herself in the mirror. Her hair was mussed, her lipstick gone, her cheeks rosy. "Oh, dear," she murmured.

Drake gave her a glance filled with obvious male satisfaction. "You look like a woman who has recently been rather thoroughly kissed."

Seeing his smile, she realized he looked the same with his hair tousled and half his shirt still unfastened.

"Where is this leading?" she questioned, voicing her worries.

"You know," he said quietly.

Thirteen

Maya woke slowly. She stretched luxuriantly, feeling truly rested. And happy in a way she hadn't been in a long time.

She and Drake and Marissa had spent every waking moment together over the weekend. Drake had been attentive, teasing her, playing with the baby and generally making himself useful. A couple of times he'd stolen a kiss, his hands and mouth gentle and enticing. Drake as smitten lover and supportive father was hard to resist.

How wonderful everything could be, if...

She wasn't sure what the "if" was comprised of, only that she felt the implied doubt of the word. For a second, she was saddened, then glancing out the window, she saw the sky was bright. Morning. She'd slept all night.

Throwing the covers off, she rose and went to the bassinet. The baby still slept, looking as sweet as an angel. Marissa hadn't awakened for the usual five-o'clock feeding.

Aware of her full breasts, Maya headed for the bathroom. She washed and dressed, then went to the kitchen. Her heart knocked a bit at finding Drake there. So was her mom and a new girl who was helping out for a few days.

Her mother introduced Maya to Elaine, a college student who was taking some time off her studies to explore the country. This was her first trip to northern California.

"Welcome to our end of the world," Maya said, pouring a cup of coffee and a large glass of milk.

"Thanks. Drake has been telling me about the coast along here. It's scary to drive Highway One, all those twists and turns and ups and downs."

Elaine looked like a California girl—all long legs and waist-length blond-streaked hair with the fresh-scrubbed, tanned face of an outdoors person—but her accent was pure Southern magnolia. She was from Kentucky.

Listening to the girl, who was about her age, talk about the adventures she'd had while traveling around the States, Maya suddenly felt her own provincialism. She'd never been anywhere farther south than San Francisco and north up to Ashland, Oregon, for the Shakespeare plays. Once her family had gone to Crater Lake to picnic and admire the scenery on a day trip.

When Inez left the kitchen and went to her own

house, Maya felt very much the outsider as the other two continued chatting about their adventures.

Drake laughed at Elaine's stories and, at her urging, told of some of his own travails in his trips around the world. The two yakked like old friends catching up with each other's lives while Elaine washed pots and cleaned up the kitchen after breakfast for the house staff and ranch help.

"Excuse me," Maya murmured after eating half a bagel. She was aware of Drake's quick glance as she put her dishes in the dishwasher, then retreated to her own room.

There, she slumped into the rocker and faced the truth. She was jealous of the young woman who'd traveled all over, carefree and confident that she would be able to make her way anywhere she went. Drake had obviously found Elaine interesting and entertaining.

Maya pressed a hand between her aching breasts. She no longer felt young, and she hadn't been carefree since she was a teenager and started sitting with the youngest Colton boys. With a grimace at her own insecurities, she rose and went to the sleeping baby.

A child certainly changed one's perspective. Marissa was barely three weeks old, but Maya acknowledged the loneliness of responsibility and knew she had only herself to blame. She and Drake could have been married by now.

Would she then have been jealous of the lovely, carefree woman who roamed the world as she wished?

There's no place in my life for a wife...

She swallowed the searing agony that rose to choke her. In truth, he hadn't wanted *her,* but that didn't mean he might not meet someone—Elaine or a young woman like her—at a future date and want that person for a wife.

Drake knocked, then entered the room when she called, "Come in."

His keen gaze searched her face. "What's wrong?" he asked quietly, coming to her. He glanced at the baby. "Is Marissa all right?"

"Yes. I was just…"

She couldn't think of an explanation for what she was doing—standing by the bassinet and feeling miserable.

"Just feeling sorry for myself, I think," she admitted with wry honesty.

He looked puzzled. "Why?"

She shrugged. "It sounds fun, traveling about and having adventures."

Understanding dawned. He shook his head, his gaze surprisingly tender. "You aren't that kind of person. You belong here. I imagine Elaine's parents worry about her a lot. She admits she rarely thinks of calling them. You would never do that to the people you love."

She thought of the months when he hadn't called or written. His words only made her more miserable. When did love become crazy and exciting like in songs?

Last summer, she answered. Then it had been moonlight and magic. Now, there were the consequences. She loved Marissa, but life was more difficult now.

Drake lifted his hand, ran a finger over her chin and lips, then spoke softly, "I realized, listening to her, how selfish and uncaring that attitude is. I thought I was being noble to leave you, but now I wonder…"

"Perhaps you were wise to go," she suggested, ignoring the terrible hurt his words caused as he stopped speaking and stared at her thoughtfully.

"Or perhaps I was scared," he corrected, his tone going hard. "Elaine flunked out of school, it turns out, and her parents are furious with her. Maybe, like her, I find it easier to take off rather than face my failures."

Startled, Maya gazed at him, wondering what in the world he meant. "You've never failed at anything."

His expression was one of tender remorse. "I've failed with you. I lost your trust. I'm sorry for that. You needed me, and I wasn't there for you." He gave a snort of bitter laughter. "It's what I'm good at— getting others into trouble while I escape scot-free."

A sense of responsibility, that was what he felt for her, she realized. He felt he'd failed her as he failed his twin so long ago, running his bike off the road while Michael, riding behind him, hadn't had time to react.

"I'm not a child, Drake. I made my own decision about what happened between us last summer. You didn't seduce or force me into an affair. You're not responsible—"

"The hell I'm not!" He shook his head angrily. "I took part in our lovemaking, then ducked out, leaving a note guaranteed to keep you at bay. I know your pride. I knew my leaving like that would end the relationship. I meant for it to."

She turned away, unable to look at him while he tore her heart to shreds.

"I thought it was for the best," he finished grimly. "I was wrong."

"It doesn't matter," she told him, weary of emotions and yearning and impossible things. She didn't want guilt and recriminations. She wasn't going to get happiness, so why continue the discussion?

"It does to me. I want to make up for that. I want to make it right between us. Like it was for that one magical week in June."

The ache was unbearable. She shook her head, denying it, him, all the wild sweet passion they had shared, the love she'd thought they'd found.

"It can't be like that, not ever again. We can't go back, Drake. It's impossible." She faced him bravely. "It's impossible," she repeated.

The muscles clenched in his jaw. His eyes were stormy and dangerous, filled with a bitterness that made her ache for him, plus anger and a refusal to accept her words.

"We can't go back," he agreed in a hoarse voice, "but we can go forward. We have to. There's the child to think of. She needs both of us."

"I won't deny you your place in her life."

He spun away and paced the room as if marshaling his arguments, then he stopped by the door. His smile was raw and unexpected. "So you can't forgive me. I realize now that I was counting on that. You always had the tenderest heart. I think that's the hardest part of all to accept. I hurt my friend...and I'll never forgive myself for that."

He left quietly, slipping out the door without a sound, like a departing ghost.

Maya breathed out shakily, not sure where they were now or how any of this could work out. Her too-full breasts reminded her that she needed to feed the baby. Bending over the little bed, she called softly, "Hey, little one, your mommy needs you to wake up."

When she lifted the child, she knew at once something was very, very wrong. Marissa's skin was hot to the touch. Very hot. She opened her eyes, but the action was listless, as if she didn't care if she ever opened them again.

Grabbing the digital thermometer from off the dresser, Maya checked the baby's temperature. Gasping, she clutched the baby to her chest and ran for the door. While she and Drake had been quarreling, their baby had lain in bed, neglected and ill.

"Drake," she cried, running to the patio. "Drake!"

He was halfway across the lawn to the beach stairs. The wind coldly snatched his name from her lips and tossed it behind her. She clutched the baby and ran desperately toward him, fear lending wings to her feet.

"Drake!"

He turned around, saw her and ran back to meet her.

"The baby," she said. "She's running a fever."

"How much?"

"A hundred and four. We have to get to the hospital."

He nodded grimly. Taking her arm, they both ran. He beat her to his truck. Opening the door, he scooped her inside, then ran around and slid in the driver's side.

"Why didn't you tell me she was sick?" he demanded.

"I didn't know," she admitted. "I thought she was just sleeping a long time. She missed the five o'clock feeding. When I decided to wake her after you left, I found she was burning up."

"Could she have gotten hold of something?"

"No. I don't think so. She seemed okay last night. She didn't eat much, but I didn't think— She must have been getting ill then. I didn't notice. I should have checked her temperature. I should have done that when I first woke and realized she'd slept so long. I—"

"Hush," he said. "Don't go blaming yourself. I didn't notice anything different about her, either."

Maya was silent for the rest of the ride to the emergency room. She heard Drake's soothing words, but she didn't believe them. She was at fault. She should have noticed her baby was sick.

"Strep throat," the pediatrician said cheerfully. "It can come on fast with babies. She'll be fine. You can take her home as soon as the office finishes the paperwork. The nurse will bring you some samples of a fever reducer. Use it if her temperature goes up again.''

Maya listened without taking her eyes off the baby. When they'd arrived at the local hospital, their regular pediatrician was making his rounds. He'd examined Marissa, nodded wisely when he'd peered into her mouth—that had made her whimper—then he'd ordered an IV. The drip tube had looked ominous as the nurse attached it to the tiny body. At noon, the doctor had checked her again and said she was ready to go home.

"Thank you," Drake said to the doctor when he left them alone in the room with its double cribs. The other baby bed was empty.

Maya sat beside the crib, her hand through the railing so she could touch the baby. Marissa instinctively clutched her mother's finger as she slept deeply.

"I've never seen her so still," Maya said in a soft voice. "It's almost as if she's…" She couldn't bring herself to say "dead."

"She's resting," Drake assured her. "She'll be okay."

Maya closed her eyes briefly, then looked at him. "No thanks to me. I should have noticed she wasn't feeling well last night. She didn't want to eat. It must have hurt to swallow, but I didn't notice."

Drake put his hands on Maya's shoulders, meaning only to soothe her, but lingering because it felt just plain good to touch her. "Hey, it's okay. Parents are human, too," he told her, trying for a lighter note.

But watching her as she kept her eyes glued to the

crib, he knew words wouldn't replace the guilt she felt.

"She might have died," Maya went on doggedly. "And I wouldn't have noticed because I was too busy being jealous of you having fun with some female you just met."

Her confession hit his heart like individual flaming arrows of pain. He knelt beside her, worry eating at him. He and Maya had been caught up in their concerns, but they hadn't neglected the baby.

"You never have to be jealous of anyone. Don't you know you're the only woman in the whole world as far as I'm concerned?"

She shook her head.

Pain filling his chest, Drake bowed his head and rested his cheek on her temple. He'd hurt her in ways he could only guess at when he'd left her alone, with only that cruel note of explanation, to face the consequences of their brief time together.

He forced himself to face the truth. Because of his fear of loving someone, because he knew how it felt to be left behind with nothing but that love, because love came with hopes and fears and dreams attached, he'd denied any chance of a future between them. He'd run from the greatest happiness he'd ever known because *he* was a coward.

"Forgive me," he said. "You have to forgive me."

Giving him a baffled glance, Maya stood when the nurse came in. So did Drake.

"I need a signature," the older woman said. "Just sign your life away right here." She handed the forms to Drake with a bright smile, then checked Marissa. "What a little doll. Is she a good baby?"

"Yes," Maya said. "She hardly ever cries."

"My granddaughter had a lot of trouble with strep throat when she was little," the nurse continued. "We had her tonsils taken out when she was three. Her temperature would shoot up just like that." She snapped her fingers. "I hope this little one isn't going to go through that, but when they start this early..." She shook her head, then smiled. "It's only the first of the crises you can expect."

Laughing as if this were a huge joke, the woman checked the papers, instructed them on the use of some medicine packets she gave them, then ushered them out.

In the truck, going back to the ranch, Maya sighed. Drake cast her a quick glance. She was vulnerable at present. Maybe it wasn't a good time to talk.

At the house, he carried the baby in the infant seat into Maya's bedroom, then stood silently while Maya tucked the tiny girl into her bed and pushed it into the corner near her desk. She lowered the blinds so the room was in semidarkness.

"I'll get us some coffee," he volunteered. In the kitchen, he recalled they'd had no lunch. Elaine was there, peeling a mound of potatoes under Inez's watchful eye.

"Hi," she said, her smile bright.

Drake spoke automatically, then explained to Inez about the baby. Clucking, she prepared sandwiches and fruit, then sent him back with a tray.

"Tell Maya not to worry about the boys," she told

him. "I'll look after them when they get home from school."

"Thanks."

He hurried to Maya. "Lunch," he said.

She hovered over the bassinet. "I'm not hungry."

"Then you can watch me eat."

He cleared a space and set the meal on her desk. Taking her arm, he guided her to a seat and put half a sandwich in her hand. "Eat. You need to produce milk."

When she managed an indignant glare, he was relieved. "You make me sound like a cow," she grumbled, taking the sandwich unwillingly.

After eating, he set the tray in the hall, something he wouldn't have ordinarily done, but it was time to talk.

Taking the chair beside her desk, he gazed at Maya. Her hair was held behind her ears with a stretchy band in deep gold. It matched the sweater she wore. Black slacks and a gambler's vest with a black satin back and gold and black brocade front completed the outfit.

She wore no makeup, but the freshness of her complexion needed no added color.

"I've always thought you were the most beautiful female I've ever known. You never had an awkward stage, but went directly from a child to a woman at some point. I don't know when. I wasn't looking."

She flashed him an incredulous glance, then turned her velvety brown gaze back to the baby.

"I know when I noticed, though," he continued, needing to get through this, to get it all said. "The year you were seventeen. I came home, saw you and didn't sleep the rest of my stay. Luckily, you were with Joe and Teddy all the time; otherwise, I might not have been able to resist—''

He paused, visions of her at that time segueing into images of her as she'd been at his father's birthday party last June. She'd worn a white dress with a lace jacket and pink roses in her hair.

His heart thudded loudly, reminding him of that first moment, when he'd walked out on the patio and there she'd been, arranging flowers around the huge birthday cake. He'd known... In that one moment, he'd known.

"Last summer..."

She dropped her head a bit so he couldn't see her eyes, and he recalled it was a mannerism she had when she didn't want him to read her thoughts.

"Last summer," he began again, "it was hopeless. As soon as I saw you, I knew how it was going to be for us. And it was," he ended softly.

Maya bit the inside of her lip to hold back the cry of protest that rose to her throat. "It isn't fair to re-mind me of how foolish we were."

"It wasn't foolish," he said in a slightly harder tone before his voice softened again. "It was won-derful and inevitable and meant to be. Neither of us could have stopped at that point."

She sighed, knowing he spoke true. Even knowing what was to come—his leaving, the painful discovery of the note, the realization that she was expecting— she would still have gone to him, into his arms, shar-ing his hot, wild kisses.

A low moan of pain and hunger and a hundred other things pushed through her clenched teeth.

He pulled his chair closer to hers so that their knees nearly touched. "As of this morning, I've been home a month. When I arrived, I fully expected to be a married man within a day, two at the most. I had planned it all out as if it was part of a campaign." He laughed without humor. "The first clue that things weren't going to go as I thought was finding you on a runaway horse. From there, it got worse."

"Drake, I need to study."

"Why? Didn't you ace your final exam?"

"Yes. I don't feel up to arguing with you."

"Then don't. Just listen. You were right about me and the past. I learned to live with Michael's death because I had to, but it was always there inside me, lingering like a festering wound, ready to break open at any moment."

"When happiness got too close," she said, intuitively knowing this was true.

"Yes. Last summer, with you, was the closest thing to total bliss I've ever known. Then I panicked and ran."

The sorrow of it came back to her, as fresh as the moment joy fled and agony started. "It was such a shock, waking and finding you gone."

"I said I wanted to save you pain, but it was myself I was protecting. If I lost you... If you came with me and something happened... It was a chance I couldn't take."

She saw the shadows race through his eyes like ghosts he couldn't shake.

He touched her cheek, then withdrew. "I've learned something this month. No one can predict life. You can't avoid it either by evasion or planning because you can't foresee bee stings or a child's illness." He gestured toward the sleeping baby.

Maya's breasts contracted, and she felt the familiar release of milk at his mention of the child. Her heart reacted in sympathy, contracting with hopeless longing as he explained why they had no future. As if she needed to hear it again. Wearily, she waited for him to finish.

"Or falling in love," he added softly. "My fate was sealed the moment I saw you. I walked across the patio to stand beside you. I've never left your side, not even when I was in a thousand miles away. You were there because you were in my heart, filling it with crazy, impossible dreams."

"Drake, please, you don't have to explain. I know you have to leave."

He dropped to his knees and slipped his arms around her waist. "Never," he vowed. "I never intend to leave you again. If you'll give me another chance." He looked deeply into her eyes. "I need you, sweet Maya, as a friend, a confidante and as my wife. Will you come with me, live with me and share whatever the future brings?"

"Why?" She really didn't understand what was suddenly different, but she knew something was. There was tension in Drake, yes, but there was something else—a sorrow coupled with a quiet expectation that she could detect but not explain.

Taking a deep breath, he told her, "I've let the past go. You were right. It was something I needed to do."

"How?" she whispered.

"Listening to you blame yourself for Marissa's illness, I realized how ridiculous that was. As if you were personally accountable for every danger that might cross her path. Sitting in the hospital I realized something else—that it wasn't my fault that I reacted quickly when that car came speeding around the curve. Michael didn't. He froze."

Looking at the terrible sadness in Drake's expression, Maya knew he was at last saying farewell to his twin. Her heart went out to him. Bending forward, she cradled his head against her breasts, offering him what comfort she could as he made this journey from the past to the present.

"He didn't run off the road into the ditch as I did. He simply stared at the car as it came at him. I think…I think I never forgave *him* for that. I couldn't forgive him for dying."

"You'd never been apart, and he left you behind," she murmured, understanding the loneliness he must have felt.

"Yes." Drake swallowed hard, then nodded toward the bassinet. "I want the promise of life she represents. She's our pledge to the future, yours and mine. Our future. I want that. I wasn't ready to admit it last June, but I am now. I want our children, how many you're willing to give me. Most of all, I want you."

With trembling hands, Maya cupped his face. She saw the truth in the depths of his gold-flecked eyes.

"I love you with all my heart," he said. "All of it. Marry me and I'll show you just how much."

She wanted to! So much! "What about the SEALs and your career with them?"

"If you don't mind living on or near the base, we'll have six months to figure out what comes next. Can you finish your studies by e-mail?"

"Everything but the final exams."

"I think we can arrange to be in San Francisco when the time comes. Marriage?"

She nodded, too choked with emotion to speak.

He laughed softly, lifted her into his arms, swung them around in a dizzy circle, then fell into the rocking chair, which creaked indignantly at being treated in such a rough fashion.

"I love you," he whispered, then simply gazed at her.

"I love you, too." She hugged him tightly. "I've always loved you."

"Lucky me."

Then he kissed her as if there were no tomorrow, until they were both breathless and filled with longing. Just when things were becoming unbearably interesting, they heard a whimper, then a full-fledged cry.

"The future speaks," he said, lifting his head, his eyes alight with the fire of passion.

And joy, she thought, as she went and lifted the hungry baby. She changed Marissa's diaper, then settled in Drake's lap in the rocker when he opened his arms to them.

They were silent while the baby nursed. Maya, unable to keep from stealing glances at her beloved, marveled at how easy it all seemed at this moment.

The future would bring its own worries and pain and dark moments, but there would be happiness, too.

As if reading her mind, Drake murmured, "We can make it. The past is important. It's there to be learned from. That's what we have to remember. To learn and go forward."

"Yes. I think our daughter will be a good reminder of that fact. Children rush headlong into life. We'll have to keep up."

With a satisfied smile, Drake wrapped his arms around her and the baby. "We will," he promised.

Sitting quietly together, he felt Maya relax and drift into sleep. Marissa also slept. Through the window, Drake watched the shadows lengthen into late afternoon. On the path to the creek where he used to while away summer days, he saw a boy on a bike, a fishing pole strapped to the rear fender.

Drake blinked in surprise, wondering who it was.

The boy stopped at the top of the hill and turned. Drake stopped rocking and sat very still. The boy smiled at him, his dark hair blowing in the winter breeze, his eyes flashing golden in the sun. Then, with a wave, he rode on, over the hill and out of sight.

Drake swallowed hard. "Goodbye," he whispered. "Good fishing."

"What?" Maya asked sleepily.

"Nothing. I love you."

He held her close and felt her warmth spreading all the way down inside him, past the longing, the need, the hunger. Past the fear, right into the very heart of him. Right into his soul.

The baby stirred and made little sucking sounds. Maya sighed against his throat. Drake scrubbed the hot sting of tears from his eyes. Michael's future was somewhere out there, beyond the hills, but his was here, with his two loves. It was the future he wanted.

* * * * *

*Read more about the Colton family saga
in TAKING ON TWINS by Carolyn Zane
coming in January 2002!*

One

Later that evening, dinner with his family sent memories cascading through Wyatt, making him feel more alive than he'd felt in years. There was nothing like the praise—and good-natured insults—of family. It was too bad that ''Meredith'' had pleaded headache and missed most of the festivities. When she'd made her excuses and stepped from the room, he'd exchanged meaningful glances with Rand and Lucy and wondered how many others at the table suspected that Meredith wasn't actually…Meredith. A good number of the family was beginning to suspect.

Several of the ''servants'' marked Meredith's exit and Wyatt was relieved to note that the security crew was still on the ball.

If Meredith was missed, it didn't dampen the festivities for long. There were toasts to the bride and groom, trips down memory lane, and a feeling of something so incredibly right. Again, Wyatt yearned for more than a professionally decorated and cleaned condo to come home to at night.

After the candles had burned low, some of the crowd retired, some headed for the hot-tub, some for the pool tables and others for after-dinner drinks in the lanai. Lucy and Rand walked with Wyatt to their neighboring suites and stepped inside Wyatt's room for a moment.

"What now?" Wyatt asked.

Rand patted the pocket that held the papers that Austin's courier had delivered that afternoon. "We need to get this information to Emily." Rand glanced at Lucy. "I'll be back in time for the wedding."

"You're leaving?" Wyatt asked.

"Have to. We can't leave Emily twisting in the wind. The more we keep her in the loop, the safer she'll be."

Frustrated by feelings of helplessness, Wyatt nodded. "Right. How did you figure out where she went?"

"Austin's P.I. found her a few hours ago." Rand paused and looked into his foster brother's eyes before he spoke. "She's in Keyhole."

Tiny hairs stood up on the back of Wyatt's neck and he froze. Had he misunderstood? *"Keyhole?* Keyhole, Wyoming? You're kidding!"

"I thought that place might ring a bell for you." Rand narrowed his eyes, searching Wyatt's face.

"What rings a bell? Why?" Lucy's head swiveled back and forth between the two men as they talked over her head. "Why would some town named Keyhole ring a bell?"

"Emily's hiding out in Keyhole?" Wyatt asked, ignoring Lucy. "Why Keyhole?"

"Don't know. The P.I. didn't talk to her. Keyhole's not far from Nettle Creek, where Dad grew up, so I guess Emily maybe feels a little less homesick." He shot a pointed look at Wyatt. "Isn't Keyhole where Annie lives now?"

"Who's Annie?" Lucy wondered.

Wyatt gave his throat a noisy clearing in hopes that he didn't sound as screwed-up as he felt. "Yeah. As far as I know."

Lucy sighed. "Hello? Guys? Remember me? Who is Annie?"

"How long has it been since you two saw each other?"

"Not since college." Wyatt passed a hand over his forehead and rubbed at the familiar ache that settled in his brow every time he thought of the life Annie led without him. Just speaking about her marriage turned him into a melancholy mess. "She got married and had a couple of kids. Twin boys, I hear."

"I'm gathering somebody named Annie has twin boys. Don't feel like you owe me any explanation or anything. After all, I'm just *standing here.*" Lucy fumed.

"Wasn't her husband killed in an accident of some kind a few years back?" Rand asked.

"Yeah. I thought you told me that."

Rand shrugged. "Can't remember."

"Maybe it was Austin." Unfortunately, Wyatt

hadn't learned of the accident that took her husband's life until long after the funeral, and by then, his condolences seemed untimely. Misplaced. At least that was the excuse he used to explain away his fears of contacting Annie. "Anyway, as far as I know she hasn't remarried."

With a moan, Lucy buried her face in her hands. "I'm invisible."

Rand laughed. "Lucy, honey, Annie was Wyatt's first—" he arched a brow at Wyatt "—and only, I believe—love."

Lucy peeped between her fingers. "*You* were in *love* once?"

"You don't need to sound so shocked."

"Excuse me? Mr. 'I-Don't-Need-Nobody-Nohow-Never' was once in love? Oh, baby. This is juicy." She hooted, then her eyes narrowed and she gently probed his cheekbones with her fingertips. "And, by the little flush in your cheeks, may I deduce that she still has your heart?"

Wyatt looked askance at Rand. "How do you put up with her meddling?"

Rand laughed. "With Lucy, it's an art form. Her talent at digging up dirt is one of the main reasons I fell in love with her."

"Aw, honey. You're so sweet." Lucy stepped into her husband's arms and tugged his mouth to hers for a solid kiss. Soon, happy moans were rumbling from their throats.

Wyatt rolled his eyes. "Don't you two have a room of your own?" he groused. For crying in the night. Sometimes they could be so obnoxious. Not to mention thoughtless. It wasn't like he had anyone of his own to turn to when they skipped off to their room to do whatever came naturally to newlyweds.

"Honey," Lucy nuzzled Rand's neck, "why are *you* going to Keyhole? Don't you think we should make Wyatt go? After all he has more reasons to go than you do, don't you think? Besides, I don't want you to go. Don't go. Pleeease? Stay with me. I'll make it worth your while..."

"I can't think straight with you kissing my ear that way," Rand groaned.

"That's it. Get out of here," Wyatt ordered and, striding to the door, yanked it open.

With one smooth move, Rand lifted Lucy and carried her to the hall.

"Don't worry, Wyatt," Lucy called. "You can be back in time for Liza's wedding. Bring a date back with you!"

Their laughter echoed down the hall and into their suite. And then, it was silent.

THE COLTONS

If you missed the first six exciting stories from
THE COLTONS, here's a chance
to order your copies today!

0-373-38704-0	BELOVED WOLF by Kasey Michaels	$4.50 U.S.☐ $5.25 CAN.☐
0-373-38705-9	THE VIRGIN MISTRESS by Linda Turner	$4.50 U.S.☐ $5.25 CAN.☐
0-373-38706-7	I MARRIED A SHEIK by Sharon De Vita	$4.50 U.S.☐ $5.25 CAN.☐
0-373-38707-5	THE DOCTOR DELIVERS by Judy Christenberry	$4.50 U.S.☐ $5.25 CAN.☐
0-373-38708-3	FROM BOSS TO BRIDEGROOM by Victoria Pade	$4.50 U.S.☐ $5.25 CAN.☐
0-373-38709-1	PASSION'S LAW by Ruth Langan	$4.50 U.S.☐ $5.25 CAN.☐

(limited quantities available)

TOTAL AMOUNT	$ _____
POSTAGE & HANDLING	$ _____
($1.00 for one book, 50¢ for each additional)	
APPLICABLE TAXES*	$ _____
TOTAL PAYABLE	$ _____

(check or money order—please do not send cash)

To order, send the completed form, along with a check or money order for the total above, payable to **THE COLTONS**, to: In the U.S.: 3010 Walden Avenue, P.O. Box 9077, Buffalo, NY 14269-9077; In Canada: P.O. Box 636, Fort Erie, Ontario L2A 5X3.

Name: _____

Address: _____ City: _____

State/Prov.: _____ Zip/Postal Code: _____

Account # (if applicable) : _____075 CSAS

*New York residents remit applicable sales taxes.
  Canadian residents remit applicable GST and provincial taxes.

Visit Silhouette at www.eHarlequin.com
COLTBACK-6

CALL THE ONES YOU LOVE OVER THE HOLIDAYS!

Save $25 off future book purchases when you buy any four Harlequin® or Silhouette® books in October, November and December 2001,

PLUS

receive a phone card good for 15 minutes of long-distance calls to anyone you want in North America!

WHAT AN INCREDIBLE DEAL!

Just fill out this form and attach 4 proofs of purchase (cash register receipts) from October, November and December 2001 books, and Harlequin Books will send you a coupon booklet worth a total savings of $25 off future purchases of Harlequin® and Silhouette® books, AND a 15-minute phone card to call the ones you love, anywhere in North America.

Please send this form, along with your cash register receipts
as proofs of purchase, to:
In the USA: Harlequin Books, P.O. Box 9057, Buffalo, NY 14269-9057
In Canada: Harlequin Books, P.O. Box 622, Fort Erie, Ontario L2A 5X3
Cash register receipts must be dated no later than December 31, 2001.
Limit of 1 coupon booklet and phone card per household.
Please allow 4-6 weeks for delivery.

**I accept your offer! Enclosed are 4 proofs of purchase.
Please send me my coupon booklet
and a 15-minute phone card:**

Name: _____

Address: _____ City: _____

State/Prov.: _____ Zip/Postal Code: _____

Account Number (if available): _____

097 KJB DAGL
PHQ4013

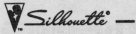

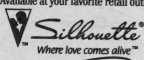

THE COLTONS

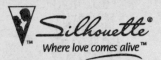

Silhouette®

Where love comes alive™

If you've enjoyed getting to know **THE COLTONS**,
Silhouette® invites you to come back and
visit the Colton family!

Just collect three (3) proofs of
purchase from the backs of three (3) different
COLTONS titles and receive a free **COLTONS**
book that's not currently available in retail outlets!

Just complete the order form and send it, along with three
(3) proofs of purchase from three (3) different **COLTONS**
titles, to: **THE COLTONS**, P.O. Box 9047, Buffalo, NY
14269-9047, or P.O. Box 613, Fort Erie, Ontario L2A 5X3.

(No cost for shipping and handling.)

- -

Name: _____

Address: _____ City: _____

State/Prov.: _____ Zip/Postal Code: _____

Please specify which title(s) you would like to receive:

❑ 0-373-38716-4 *PROTECTING PEGGY* by Maggie Price
❑ 0-373-38717-2 *SWEET CHILD OF MINE* by Jean Brashear
❑ 0-373-38718-0 *CLOSE PROXIMITY* by Donna Clayton
❑ 0-373-38719-9 *A HASTY WEDDING* by Cara Colter

Remember—for each title selected, you must send three (3)
original proofs of purchase. To receive *all four (4)* titles, just send
in all twelve (12) proofs of purchase.

(Please allow 4-6 weeks for delivery.
Offer good while quantities last.
Offer available in Canada and the U.S. only.)
(The proof of purchase should be cut off the ad.)

THE COLTONS
ONE PROOF OF PURCHASE
COLTPOP-R2